A DEATH FOR KING AND COUNTRY

Euphemia is returning from a visit to New York on April 12th on the RMS *Carpathia*, when an emergency signal sends the ship rushing to the aid of the sinking RMS *Titanic*. By the time the *Carpathia* arrives, the *Titanic* has sunk. Euphemia and Richenda give up their cabins and help the few survivors. On their return to shore, a personal wire is sent to Euphemia from a government department asking her to confirm whether or not the enigmatic spy Fitzroy is among the survivors. He is not. Then a letter arrives from Fitzroy headed 'In the Event of my Death', which opens up a whole new adventure...

A DEATH FOR KING AND COUNTRY

A DEATH FOR KING AND COUNTRY

by

Caroline Dunford

Magna Large Print Books
Long Preston, North Yorkshire,
BD23 4ND, England.

British Library Cataloguing in Publication Data.

Dunford, Caroline
    A death for king and country.

    A catalogue record of this book is
    available from the British Library

    ISBN   978-0-7505-4235-7

    10\1\6

First published in Great Britain in 2015 by Accent Press Ltd.

Published in Large Print 2016 by arrangement with
Accent Press Ltd.

Magna Large Print is an imprint of Library Magna Books Ltd.

Printed and bound in Great Britain by
T.J. (International) Ltd., Cornwall, PL28 8RW

Chapter One

The Night of April 14th 1912

Richenda and I leaned as far as we dared over the railing and peered out into the vast, starlit sea. The air was so cold it was like pressing our faces against a sheet of ice. The inkiness of the night blurred the line between the sea and the sky. We could have been sailing off the end of the world. The frivolity and liveliness we had found in the week we had spent in New York now seemed a lifetime away.

'Do you think we will see the lights soon?' asked Richenda for the thousandth time. I could not berate her for her repetition, for the very same thought was echoing around in my own mind. I looked at my wristwatch, a bridesmaid's present from Richenda and Hans, but I could not read the dial.

'It's too dark to see,' I said, 'but the Captain did say it would take six hours to get there. And that was with turning off the heating and our lights.'

'Can you believe it?' scowled Richenda. 'I heard the woman in the cabin next to ours complaining about the cold. And she with six mink coats, too!'

Despite the seriousness of the situation, I felt pleasure at my companion's remark. It would not have been that long ago she would have made such a complaint herself. Only a year ago, Richenda

Stapleford had been an almost entirely self-centred, spoiled woman, obsessed with fashion, who at best turned a blind eye to the actions of her malevolent twin Richard. Now, recently married to the banker Hans Muller in what was essentially a marriage of convenience for them both, she had unexpectedly blossomed. Having been her house-maid, and now paid companion, we had shared many exploits together. The damage done to her by a harsh stepmother, an uncaring father, and a manipulative twin had been worn away to reveal a good woman.

A woman who, like myself, was currently fretting and praying over those hundreds of souls at peril on the sea tonight.

There was an aspect of 'there but for the grace of God go we' about the situation. When Hans had declared his intention of a spectacular world cruise for Richenda and himself, she had begged to go on the RMS *Titanic*. Hans had demurred, not at the cost (although it would have been steep even for him), but at the declaration that the ship was practically unsinkable.

'I cannot believe such a thing,' he had said. 'I fear the crew and Captain will take greater risks if they believe themselves invincible. It is the nature of man to do so.'

Richenda had argued hard, but for once Hans had refused her. If he had not, we too would be amongst the stricken passengers of the flounder-ing *Titanic*, rather than on board the RMS *Car-pathia*, racing to rescue her. We had no idea what had happened, but like many of those on board we had volunteered to share our quarters with

10

those about to be rescued. The *Carpathia* was not the biggest of ships, and the *Titanic* had, we believed, almost two thousand souls on board. Hans, like many of the men, had given up his bed completely. Richenda was to share my accommodation and he would sleep on deck, their entire stateroom suite given up. For Hans there had been no question that this should be done, and one stern look at Richenda had convinced her of the same.

The mood among the passengers on board had been one of disbelief. Unlike Hans, no one else seemed to have thought *Titanic* sinkable. As it was, people whispered of slight damage and maybe a few people needing to leave the ship. But as the hours wore on and the Captain diverted all possible power to the engines, I think everyone began to realise the gravity of the situation.

Richenda gave a little cry and pointed out to sea. 'There!' she gasped. Ahead of us, in the distance, glimmered some indistinct object. We were quiet as we approached it, but no sooner did it seem to become firm amid the shimmering night sea than we felt the ship shift beneath our feet.

'Iceberg,' murmured a woman to my right.

Moonlight struck the structure as we passed it. I believe everyone on board held their breath. Certainly no one around us spoke for several minutes. The beauty of the sparkling ice in the night was unearthly. If was as if a piece of heaven had fallen from the skies and landed in the dark calm of the waters.

'Let's hope there were enough boats,' said Hans, appearing at our sides. He handed us each a wrap.

'They're gathering shawls for the survivors. You can wear these for now, but...'

'Of course,' I said, 'we will at once hand them over to those in more need.'

Richenda, her teeth chattering, nodded. 'It is so cold on deck, I cannot imagine how cold the water must be.'

'You would not have to imagine it for very long,' said Hans grimly. 'A few minutes at most.'

Both Richenda and I gasped at the implication. 'What did you mean about boats?' I asked. 'Are there other ships coming to the rescue?'

Hans shook his head. 'I talked to one of the officers. Other ships have answered the distress call, but even at six hours away we are by far the nearest. No, I was referring to the lifeboats.'

'What do you mean?' asked Richenda.

Hans sighed and huddled down further in his greatcoat. 'I knew how much you wanted to go on the *Titanic*, my dear, so I did explore the possibility more fully than you perhaps realised. One of the facts that decided me was the builders' declaration that a full number of lifeboats was not needed as they would never be used.'

He took Richenda's hand in his. 'I do not take risks with those I value.' He smiled at me too. Richenda blushed or at least went a shade darker in the night. As a redhead with freckles, and of a fulsome figure, blushing, to which she was unfortunately prone, was never kind to her.

'How short of places were they?' I asked.

Hans shook his head. 'It is pointless to speculate now. But I do fear the number of survivors will not overload this ship, as some have feared.'

I looked down into the dark water and shivered.

I cannot tell you how long it was from then that the *Carpathia* began to slow. I know I was colder than I had ever been in my life. However, despite Hans' prompting neither of us could bear to retire inside the ship. It was as if we both felt that by willing it so the ship would move faster through the endless sea. That and the sight of the icebergs would have had me rushing out to check every few minutes that we too were not in danger of collision.

The ship gradually slowed and slowed. Richenda and I peered into the night. 'Where is it?' she asked. And then we heard the whistles and the cries from the small wooden lifeboats that remained. 'She's gone,' I said. My heart felt like a stone within me. 'The entire ship has gone. We are too late.'

We were not late. To this day people speak of the *Carpathia* and the impossible race her captain made across the sea. The speed we achieved was incredible, but the damage done to the *Titanic* by the iceberg was beyond anything anyone had thought possible. It seemed she had split quite in two and sunk quickly to the bottom of the sea.

The tales we heard that night will stay with me for the rest of my life. Of wives who chose to stay with their husbands. Of small children, now orphaned, handed over by third-class passengers who were refused a place on a lifeboat. Of the men who had run amok and released the lifeboats early in their fear and cowardice, and the bravery of the

13

crew who had restored order even though they knew there was no chance of their own survival. And we heard the terrible, terrible stories, of those locked below decks, and of keys never found no matter how some brave officers sought.

Richenda and I did not stay in our cabin. We helped the crew as much as we could, but more than anything we made what poor efforts we could to comfort those lost, cold, bereaved, and shocked. Hans too was out in our ship's lifeboats, scouring for any souls still clinging to wreckage or held aloft by their life-jackets. He never spoke of what he saw that night, but when he came back to us I saw the haunted look in his eyes. It also helps explain what transpired next.

Richenda, though stout in many ways, does not have my constitution. I have worked below stairs, and before that I grew up in a vicarage where exercise was praised and encouraged. Richenda, long overfond of cake, could not stay the same course I could. I found Hans, by purest chance, as he came in from the boats, and told him I was seeking his wife.

'She has been much moved by the plight of the survivors, but she is not as strong as I. She needs to rest. I fear in this cold she will make herself ill.'

Hans put a hand on my shoulder. 'You have both done more than could have been asked of you,' he said. 'And there will time for you to do more as we travel back to port, but you both need to rest.'

I looked across the sea of faces, the survivors still being sorted and shepherded to whatever shelter could be found.

'There are not as many I as thought there

14

would be,' I said sadly.

'I believe over a thousand lives have been lost,' said Hans.

I felt my knees crumble beneath me. Only Hans' strong arm around my waist stopped me falling into a dead faint.

'A thousand,' I murmured. 'A thousand.'

'I should not have told you,' said Hans. I could hear in his voice he was cross with himself.

'Was it very terrible out in the boats?' I asked.

'Come, let us find my wife,' was all he would answer.

We found Richenda sitting on the lower deck, tears streaming down her face, a child of two or three, dressed in poor clothing, clasped in her arms. Richenda rocked the child gently and was crooning to her despite her tears. When she looked up at us her face showed her shock and despair.

'Her mother died on the lifeboat,' she said. 'Her father stayed on the ship. She is two and half years old and her name is Amy.' Then she began to sob as if her heart might break.

Hans helped her to her feet, but he made no attempt to take the child from her. 'Take her to your bed,' he said. 'She is cold and scared.'

'She is the daughter of an Irish maid,' said Richenda, and I could hear the fear in her voice.

'Does she have any other relatives?' asked Hans.

'She was with another woman, who had come to know them on the journey. The woman thought not.'

'This other woman would not take her?' asked Hans.

Richenda shook her head. 'She has lost her hus-

15

band and has her two own children with her.'

Hans nodded. 'You'd better take her with you to your quarters. You both need rest, and Amelia needs to be out of this cold.'

Richenda looked at him warily. He gave her a gentle push towards the cabins. 'Go and rest. There is nothing more to be done now.'

I let Richenda go on ahead. 'I have never seen her like that,' I said to Hans.

'Tonight has changed us all,' said Hans.

'The child,' I said haltingly, 'I fear she will not easily give her up.'

Hans looked down at me. 'If the child has no other relatives I see no reason why she should,' he said somewhat fiercely.

I must have looked surprised. 'Honestly, Euphemia,' he said, 'I would have thought you knew me better. An accident of birth is no reason to discriminate against a small child, and an orphaned one at that.'

I always knew Hans Muller was a good man, but it was that night I realised how very good he was.

16

Chapter Two

In which the British Government unexpectedly calls on my aid in a most unpleasant manner

Richenda stayed in her cabin from that point onwards. Not because of a lack of desire to help, but because without any previous experience she had suddenly become the mother of a sad, confused, and exceedingly demanding toddler.

It transpired that Richenda had actually seen the dead mother brought aboard, with the child still in her arms, and it was as if she couldn't let Amy, as she insisted on being called, go a minute without being held. Apart from seeing that she had what she needed for the child Hans let her be. He knew she was afraid he would take the child away, and to be fair most men would have done their best to have found the child a place among her own class. But Hans' first wife had suffered a series of miscarriages, and perhaps it was this as much as his own strength of character that made him loath to take a child from his wife's arms.

Hans is not from the upper classes, but a respectable middle-class man who has made his own fortune. Because of this he has less class sensibilities than many of his peers, and a strong feudal ethic that makes his small estate one of the best-run and happiest in the country.

But I fear if I praise Mr Muller much more it will seem as if I harbour romantic feelings towards him. I do not, but I do like him very much, and after this voyage I liked him even more. He had promised me that despite Richenda changing status from a guest in his house to his wife I would always have a home with him, and seeing how he responded to Amy made me certain for the first time that he had meant what he said.

On board the *Carpathia* I moved among the passengers, doing what I could and making as few demands upon the overstretched crew as possible. I was surprised therefore on the morning after the rescue, when I had snatched but a few hours' rest, that I was sought out by a crewman and asked to report to the wireless station.

The wireless station on board a ship is very small and almost shack-like, so I was surprised to be asked to step inside. The wireless operator and the first mate were waiting for me.

'Miss St John?' asked the first mate, offering his hand, 'I understand you and your companions have given up your stateroom. Thank you.'

'It is no more than many have done,' I answered confused, 'and so much less than I would like to be able to do.'

'Still, the attitude of passengers such as yourself is much appreciated, ma'am.'

'Thank you,' I said, preparing to leave. 'I am sure you have much more important things to do than...'

The first mate shook his head. 'No, ma'am, that's not why you were asked here. Although if I were able I would individually thank every one of you who have showed such kindness.' He paused. 'We have received a wire for you.' He frowned. 'From the British Government.'

'For me?'

He held out his hand to the wireless operator, who handed him a slip of paper.

'"To be conveyed in words to Miss St John only by a senior member of the crew. Please ascertain if Mr Fitzroy among the survivors from the *Titanic*. Response desired as soon as possible. Matter of utmost secrecy and urgency. Please destroy message."'

At this point the first mate put a match to the edge of the paper and did so. 'We have instructions we are to wire your response as soon as we have it, ma'am.'

'But don't you have a list of the survivors?' I asked.

'It's in hand, as is the matter of informing relatives,' said the first mate. I noticed how tired he and the wireless operator were. The former had deep shadows under his eyes, whereas the first mate standing in my presence seemed unaware that he was swaying slightly. 'I also understand from both this and another message we have received that any enquiries must be made discreetly as much as they must be made swiftly.'

'How then?' I asked.

'I believe, ma'am, that they require you to do this by sight alone.'

I made no further protestation and left the two men to their duties. I suppose I should mention at this point that Mr Fitzroy, also sometimes known as Lord Milton, is a spy for the British Empire.

Through my scandalous and seeming unbreakable habit of ending up at the scenes of crimes, and often murders, I have come into contact with Mr Fitzroy on more than one occasion. Indeed, it is arguable he once saved my life.

I certainly owed him a debt, but more than that the shadowy department for which he worked was more than aware of my true identity, as the estranged granddaughter of an earl who had been forced into service to assist her family. None of my employers had ever known who I was and I did not wish them ever to do so. It was the unspoken threat by Fitzroy's department that if I did not help them out they would reveal my identity, as much as any debt to the man, that made me embark on this difficult task. There has been no mending of the decades-long rift between by mother and her father, and accordingly I am the family's sole supporter.

What would make it harder was that I could not tell either Hans or Richenda what I was doing. I had signed a new-fangled thing called the Official Secrets Act, which prevents me on pain of many nasty and terrible things being done to me from talking about Fitzroy or his department. In similar situations past I had been in the company of others who have also signed the Act, such as Bertram, Richenda's half-brother, or Rory McLeod, a most efficient butler and my one-time ... *two*-times fiancé, and it had been somewhat easier.

I spent the rest of the day moving among the survivors, helping the crew with the delivery of food and drink, and scanning the faces of all the men. Far fewer men than women had survived. The men, apart from a few passengers from First Class who had commandeered lifeboats (and who I, having seen the suffering of those whose loved ones had nobly stayed behind, felt should be thrown back in the manner of imperfect fish) were in the main the men who had rowed the boats.

I made as sure as I could that I met all the men concerned. Fitzroy, love him or hate him, and most people did one or the other, was not a man I could imagine dead. The world would certainly be the darker for the loss of his irascible charm and quick wits. But he was also a man capable of great coldness who would sacrifice anyone or anything if his King or Country required it.

As I made my way to the wireless room once more I pondered on what Fitzroy would have done in his final hours. Would he have fought for a place on a lifeboat or would he have been one of the ones compelling the rest to order? Of all of them I imagine he would have realised the situation was dire almost at once. I liked to think that if he had wanted to get off the ship he could have done and his absence dictated that at the end he had behaved like a true gentleman and helped women and children to safety even though he knew it would cost him his life.

I delivered my message to the wireless operator and left feeling rather low.

I was somewhat surprised to receive a summons to the wireless room later in the day. As before the first mate was waiting there for me. 'I'm very sorry, ma'am,' he said, 'but we have received a further message that requires your attention.'

'What is it now?' I asked tersely. I was almost dead on my feet from fatigue.

The first mate coughed and looked uncomfortable. The wireless operator would not meet my gaze.

'Yes?' I asked imperiously.

'If I might be so bold, ma'am,' said the first mate, 'as to ask if you are sure without doubt that the man they're seeking is not among the rescuers.'

'I have made as certain as I can,' I retorted. 'Obviously the ship is vastly overcrowded, and despite the sterling efforts of your crew there is still a certain amount of chaos above and below deck.'

'You might like to check again, ma'am,' said the first mate.

'Oh, for heaven's sake!' I exclaimed. 'Is this what they want me to do?'

The first mate shook his head. 'No, ma'am. They've asked, if you are certain, if you also will check the dead before we commit any burials at sea.'

I blanched and the first mate rushed to bring me a wooden chair. I sat down.

'They want me to do what?' I said, shocked.

'Look, ma'am, if you could give me a description of this man they are so eager to find, I will check the dead men.' The first mate's accent slipped a little. 'It ain't right to be asking a lady to look at corpses.'

The operator nodded his silent approval.

I did consider it, but I knew Fitzroy had been jealous of his true identity. Besides, I owed him more than one favour that I would likely now never be able to repay. I think perhaps a small part of me knew I would only be able to accept and move on from his death when I saw his body.

I took a deep breath. 'It's all right, Officer,' I said, 'I appreciate your concern, but my father was a village vicar and I have had occasion to see the dead before.' I felt it wise not to include my over familiarity with murdered corpses at this moment.

'I don't think you understand, ma'am,' said the first mate. 'Some of these men have been in the water for some time.'

'I imagine that would change their appearance for the worse,' I said, bravely swallowing back the bile that was hitting the back of my throat.

The first mate winced. 'There has already been some deterioration in the water. Even a few fish have ... ma'am.'

A look passed between us and I understood. I managed to make it to the rail before I lost what poor lunch I had managed to snatch.

Chapter Three

A most surprising and ill-mannered visitor in excellent shoes

I shall spare you the detail of my searches, but I can say that Fitzroy was not among the dead I saw. At the time I remember thinking, between retches, how very typical of the man it was to put me through such an experience for no gain. I dreamt for weeks of what I saw, and even today I still suffer nightmares. I confess that whole experience gave me a great distaste for travelling by sea.

Fortunately, Richenda shared my misgivings. That, and the fact she appeared to have suddenly acquired a small, but passionate daughter, made a continuation of the honeymoon on to Italy, as had been planned, impossible. I think even Hans was yearning for the safety and familiarity of his home. He made promises of taking us both abroad again soon, but I believe both Richenda and I had never been happier than when we set foot once more on British soil.

We had been back at the Muller estate for three days when Amy awoke with her normal morning scream. Hans and I, always early risers, were already sitting down to breakfast. His handsome face contorted with pain as the child's cries echoed through the house. They quickly subsided and Hans who had paused mid-meal took the top off his egg with some fierceness.

'I am sure Richenda will realise that she cannot remain sleeping in the child's room,' I said.

Hans bit savagely into a piece of toast, but being a gentleman he chewed and swallowed before he spoke. 'I have offered her the choice of experienced nannies and children's nurses, who may have a better idea of how best to help Amy.'

I poured him a cup of tea, rather than the more enlivening coffee. 'Are you regretting bringing Amy back with us?' I asked gently. 'I think it unlikely Richenda would agree to give her up.'

'No, of course not,' snapped Hans. 'Though even if I were I could hardly turn the child out. She has been through more than enough.' He sighed. 'I had hoped Richenda would take better to motherhood.'

I sat bolt upright in my seat. 'That I will not allow,' I said firmly, 'Richenda is devoted to the girl and has barely left her side since she was pulled from the sea.'

'Yes, but Euphemia,' answered Hans. 'I am not at all sure that is the best way to handle a child. Was your mother by your side day and night?'

'I was encouraged towards independence,' I admitted, 'but not at the age of two.'

'At two I was in the care of nursery maids. It was a treat and a pleasure to visit my mother each day. Certainly, there was no question of my keeping my mother from my father's side. Such a thing would have been thought preposterous.'

I sensed that this was the root of the matter. Not only had Hans lost his honeymoon, he was now losing his bride. It was not a topic of which I could

25

talk openly, of course. Indeed, Hans' frustration must have been severe for him to refer to it in front of me even obliquely. I was surprised. It had hardly been a love match, but then Hans did need an heir for his estate and Richenda, though certainly not old, was not in the first bloom of youth. I suspected Hans wanted to sort out the matter of his line quickly.

I found myself blushing and became particularly attentive to my sausages.

'Do you think, Euphemia, you could try and persuade her to accept some staff to help with the child? I will give her free rein on the appointments. We cannot go on like this.'

'Of course,' I said, 'I will certainly speak to her.'

'Perhaps you could also mention that her ... er ... absence from my ... er...'

Dear God, did the man think he actually had to spell it out to me? The breakfast table was no place for the discussion of conjugal rights at the best of times – with his wife's spinster companion, it was wholly inappropriate.

Fortunately my blushes and Hans' behaviour were saved by the arrival of the Mullers' butler, Stone, a man as solid, reliable, and silent as his name.

'I apologise for the interruption, sir, madam, but there is a man, I believe a professional man not a tradesman, who desires a conversation with Miss St John. He says, and, if I may be so bold, appears, to have been travelling all night, and has a message of the utmost urgency for her.'

'Then I must see him,' I said, rising gratefully from the table.

'Do you want me to accompany you?' asked Hans, who had also risen as if I were a proper lady and not merely his wife's companion.

'No, thank you, Hans,' I said. 'I am sure Stone is more than capable of judging the man's character, and he has assured us this caller is no tradesman.'

'But he didn't call him a gentleman,' pointed out Hans.

Stone, who had been silently standing by, impassive as a monolith, spoke once more.

'I would not like to attach the title of gentleman to the caller, sir, but I believe him to be as respectable as any professional can be.'

There was the vaguest sneer over the word 'professional', for Stone, as with any good servant, regarded with unease a man who made his living by working in any other capacity.

I muttered something indistinct to them both and hurried to the morning room where I was sure Stone would have put our visitor. I did not wait for him to announce me, but showed myself in. It had occurred to me on my short trip through the house the man might be an associate of my mother and be bringing me news of her or my little brother. My mother was as keen as I that my true identity stayed hidden, and only under the direst of emergencies would she have sent me a message directly.

Awaiting me was a young man with a particularly cultivated moustache and oiled black hair, in a suit that had clearly been cut unostentatiously by the best tailors. These attributes might indeed have signalled him as a successful tradesperson, if it hadn't been for his overly long face and slight overbite, which marked him as at least related to the aristocracy if not part of its elite. As he turned towards me there was an intimation about him of the devil-may-care confidence that Fitzroy had always displayed. I recognised him for what he was at once: a man in the special service of his country. Butterflies fluttered in my stomach.

'You come from Fitzroy,' I said bluntly.

'Indeed, Miss Martins,' he said, using my real name.

'So I take it he's not dead?'

The man threw back his jacket flaps and sat down. 'Oh no, he's still quite dead.'

I gave him a hard stare. It was the height of rudeness to sit uninvited, and even more so to take his seat while I remained standing. I did not like him. I trusted him even less.

I sat down opposite him on the edge of the sofa, my back ramrod-straight as my mother had taught me. I, at least, would display proper breeding.

'Really dead or *conveniently* dead?' I asked.

The man spread out his hands in front of him in a mock-helpless manner. 'As far as I am aware he is dead. The department has had no news of him since he boarded the *Titanic*.'

'I see. How do I figure in all this?'

'That is also something I am at a loss to know,' said the young man, shifting his seat to focus his attention more intently on me. 'From our records you appear to have had no more than the mere passing acquaintance with Fitzroy.'

'Indeed,' I said coldly.

'So you weren't secretly his lover?'

I shot out of my seat. 'I have no idea why you

28

have come here, but if you are intent on nothing but insulting me I must insist you depart at once.'

The man sat back once more. 'Interesting,' he said softly. Then more boldly he added, 'I apologise unreservedly, ma'am. That Fitzroy would ask me to call upon you for this task is extraordinary. I can only surmise he held you and your abilities in the highest esteem.'

'And what task might that be?'

'Oh, didn't I say? He wants you to be his executor.'

Chapter Four

In which things become even more like a dream – and not a very nice one at that

At this point the young man, who hadn't seen fit to give me a name, not even a false one, reached down beside his chair and picked up a small attaché case. He held it out to me, forcing me to come and take it from him. As I took it, he held on for a moment. 'Are you accepting the duty to be Fitzroy's executor?' he asked.

I hesitated. A last wish is, to me, a very serious thing. 'What does it entail?' I asked.

'I have no idea. Fitzroy kept his other life very private.'

'But Mr Edward...' I said, thinking of the one man I knew he had worked alongside.

The young man shook his head.

'Whatever is in his will, he made it clear he wanted you specifically to deal with it, so I assume it must be within your capabilities if that is what is making you hesitate. He would hardly ask a civilian to do anything serious.'

I shrugged off the insult and retreated with the case. I slid the catches open and took out a small envelope. The seal had already been broken. My eyebrows rose.

The young man waved his arm about in a dismissive fashion. 'That's just the letter naming you. Everything else inside is all still sealed and intact.'

I was confident Fitzroy could have worked his way around any seal, but something about the eager anticipation in my visitor's manner suggested he did not know the contents of the will and thoroughly wished to.

Inside the case was one large packet. It was about the width and breadth of a folio case and a couple of inches thick. Pressing it between my fingers I concluded it contained only papers. A lot of papers. The packet itself was wrapped in sealed brown paper, and further wrapped with string, with a number of wax seals affixed.

On the front in large cursive script was my real name. I had no idea if it was Fitzroy's hand as I had never seen it, but it was elegant and yet precise, which reminded me of him. It was certainly secure. It seemed Fitzroy had intended to send a severe message that it was not to be opened by anyone but me.

'And if I hadn't accepted?' I asked.

'It was all to be burned unopened. He specified

that too.'

I placed the package back inside the case and pushed the catches back into place. I rose.

'Well, my thanks for delivering this to me. I will ring for Stone to show you out.'

'Aren't you going to open it?'

'I am. But not in your presence. It seems Mr Fitzroy went to a lot of effort to ensure that the contents were for my eyes only, and I intend to keep them that way.'

The young man got to his feet, tugging down the sides of his jacket in an ill-concealed display of irritation.

'I can find my own way out.'

'Considering your areas of expertise, I'm sure you will not mind if I get our butler to ensure you leave the premises.'

The young man seemed caught between flattery and feeling insulted. He struggled with his expression for a few moments and then gave a bark of laughter.

'Fair enough.'

I watched Stone escort him to his small automobile from the window. I had a good view of the drive, and I waited until he had driven out of sight. Then I waited a little longer just to be certain.

Hans was still waiting for me in the breakfast chamber, so I hurried to my room and placed the package on my dressing table. Before I left the room I checked the window was bolted shut. I didn't think he would return, but with those sorts of people one could never be sure.

Of course I would dearly have liked to open the

packet and reveal the contents, but I had already been away too long. As it was I had to think up a believable story about my visitor. At the moment I could only think of throwing Stone's reputation to the wind and saying it was indeed a tradesman trying his luck. But then I remembered Rory, who had once been butler at Stapleford Hall, telling me that it wasn't by their tailoring that he knew the upper classes from the simply rich, but by their pocket watches and above all their shoes. It would grossly unfair of me to blame Stone.

'Is everything all right?' asked Hans, looking up as I re-entered the breakfast room. 'I was all set to seek you out, but Richenda assured me you are more than equal to dealing with one gentleman.'

Richenda had indeed joined the table. She did not look well. There were bags under her eyes and her skin was sallow. She looked very, very tired, which as all women know is one of the worst looks to wear.

'Where is Amy?' I asked.

'She has gone back to sleep,' said Richenda. 'So I thought I would try to take a little breakfast.'

I slid back into my seat and signalled to Stone to bring me fresh coffee. I could see Hans beginning to bridle, so I cut in quickly before he could speak. 'Richenda, I don't think this situation can continue.'

Richenda's nostrils flared and her face took on a rosy hue. Now I had to cut her off quickly before she went into a tantrum. These are, since her marriage, happily rare, but always bad and one at breakfast can destroy the whole day. I said what I thought would be most likely to take the wind from her sails.

'I do not think it is fair to Amy.'

Only her finishing school training and the fact her mouth was full stopped Richenda's jaw from dropping. Hans watched me hopefully. He knew I had to make this good. I used an old trick of Fitzroy's of sandwiching bad news between good.

'I do not believe Amy could have a more devoted mother than yourself, Richenda. However, the child is still clearly troubled and she is exhausting you. Do you not think that to give her the best chance of a full and happy recovery we should arrange for her to both see some other children and to undertake as normal a routine as possible? Hans has offered you some new staff, and carefully selected they could perhaps make all the difference. Or perhaps you could invite Bertram to stay, and ask him to bring Merry?'

Hans' eyes lit up.

Richenda finished her mouthful slowly.

'I understand,' she said. 'I have no problem being by Amy's side day and night, but it is some weeks now and I feel I have made no real progress.'

'There is nothing more you could possibly have done,' I said quickly. I did not for a moment misjudge her intentions and I wanted her to know this. 'Naturally the child must grieve, but being as young as she is she has the capacity to bounce back.'

'Instead of insisting you dance attendance on her,' said Hans darkly. It took much restraint on my part not to kick him under the table. I glowered instead and he gave me a puzzled look.

Men can be so idiotic at times. The only way to reach Richenda was through her concern for her new obsession.

Richenda scowled at her husband, but concern for her new daughter won out.

'She has such terrible nightmares.'

'Of course she does,' I said. 'I cannot bear to imagine what she has endured, but I feel strongly that new, happy memories will overwrite the old ones, and that is what should be the focus now.'

To my delight Richenda nodded. 'You really are un-femininely intelligent, Euphemia,' she said with a smile. 'I admit I could do with some help.' Hans practically quivered with hope, but had the sense to keep his mouth shut this time. 'Perhaps you?' she said.

'No,' I said firmly. 'Merry would be infinitely better at this than me.'

'She wouldn't come without Merrit,' said Richenda.

'But that's the point,' I said excitedly. 'Merry is still working at Stapleford Hall. Bertram has gone back to White Orchards and taken Merrit with him. She hasn't seen him for weeks.' Merrit was Bertram's chauffeur, but both he and Merrit were often to be found at Bertram's family home, Stapleford Hall, as his own estate, White Orchards, regularly suffered one building calamity after another.

'Besides,' I said in an attempt to clinch it, 'isn't it time Bertram paid you a bride visit? He has yet to give you your wedding present, after all!'

'Oh, all right,' said Richenda. 'Don't think I don't realise you two have cooked this up between you. I'm going upstairs to have a rest before Amy wakes again. Euphemia may arrange all the details.'

'I will write the letters this morning,' I promised.

When she had gone Hans applauded me. 'Bravo, Euphemia! If there is anything I can do for you?'

He said this with a big smile plastered on his face, secure in the expectation that as ever I would ask for nothing.

'Actually,' I said, 'there might just be something. Family concerns mean I may require some time away from Richenda's side. I would be grateful if you could smooth that matter for me.'

Hans looked at me as if I had stuck my fork in his hand. 'That's why you wanted Merry here!' he said. 'You have become positively devious, Euphemia.'

'I prefer diplomatic,' I said with a smile. 'It's the company I've been keeping.'

Hans bowed his head, acknowledging defeat.

Chapter Five

In which the dead talk to me, and prove to have an uncomfortable sense of humour

Of course, I had first to make good my promises and write the wretched letters, one to Bertram inviting him to visit and one to the housekeeper at Stapleford Hall, Mrs Lewis, who I knew would be the person to approach, regarding Merry.

35

Lord Richard Stapleford, Richenda's twin, would have denied me simply out of spite, but with his time now split between his new estate of Peterfield and his time as an MP, he would in all likelihood have no idea where Merry was.

Mrs Lewis, a very fair woman, could arrange it easily. I knew she had the best interests of her staff at heart and while she had said she would train Merry up as a housekeeper, should she get the chance to move to the Mullers' growing household her prospects would be much improved. I proposed a loan in the first place and should the Mullers require her for more extended service I suggested Hans should make the approach to Sir Richard.

I summoned Stone and handed him my two letters, asking that they went post-haste. I had taken great care over the one to Mrs Lewis, but I fear Bertram was receiving no more than a scrawled note. My impatience to open Fitzroy's packet was so great my skin positively itched!

Hans, I knew, as he was spending time at home rather than at work in the city, would have headed down to the stables to speak with his factor and go over estate matters. He was a most dutiful master. Richenda was asleep. I had the rest of the morning to myself. I resisted the urge to run, but made my way upstairs as calmly as I could. I collected the package and took it through to the little boudoir-cum-study Hans had insisted on allotting me once it was clear I would be living at the estate long term.

'Everyone needs their private space,' he had urged, and indeed over time I had found it most restful to have my own retreat. I put the packet down on the table. It lay there unmoving. Now I had the opportunity to open it I found myself strangely reluctant. So I did what the English do in all times of confusion and ordered more tea.

Sipping my tea and lemon, I considered my reluctance. In part I ascribed it to a certain sadness that a seemingly invincible adventurer such as Fitzroy was gone, but my greater fear was what I would be asked to do. There was now no hope of declining whatever lay within the bounds of that sealed parcel. Fitzroy had displayed, on occasion, a certain dark sense of humour. He had certainly enjoyed teasing me. I had no little concern for what he might request.

Taking a small, but sharp letter opener I cut the strings and broke the seals. Inside were four large packets, each addressed to me by my pseudonym of Miss St John. They were numbered clearly one to four.

First things first. I burned the outer paper that displayed my real name in the grate. Then I turned my attention to the packets. Really, each was no more than a large letter. On the labelled one Fitzroy had written, 'On your honour, Euphemia, of which you have more than most gentlemen, I request you open these letters in order and that the next one is never opened until the tasks of the former are completed.'

I felt a little buzz of excitement. Was this some kind of strange treasure hunt? Fitzroy, I knew instinctively, would have no gold to offer, but that which he deemed far more important: Information.

37

With a shaking hand I slit open the first envelope and took out two sheets of paper. They were closely, but neatly, written.

My very dear Euphemia,

It appears I am dead. I have to say I am quite annoyed at this prospect, but please rest assured that any revenge I may hope to seek on whatever, or more likely whoever, caused my demise, I would not lay at your door.

Instead I must beg some favours that you tidy the scrambled life I have left behind. Although I believe only one of the tasks I must ask you to undertake presents any slight danger, the others will not be easy to achieve. I have therefore left what payment I can; not in money, but in information that I hope will prove useful and illuminating to you.

On completion of each task you may open the next envelope and within that you will find your reward, such as it is.

Now, I am fully aware you could open all these papers at once and read whatever I have written for you. I also know that you are aware that is the kind of thing an unscrupulous person such as myself might do, but I have always been aware you were a much better person than I.

Flattery, I hope, will get me everywhere. It certainly has been most useful in my former life. (How very strange to write former.)

I am sure you are wondering why I have chosen you. There are many reasons, but firstly, as I have indicated, I know you are burdened by both honesty and honour. Secondly, you have a remarkable mind, and if you had been born a man I am sure you would have achieved great things. For all I know you may still do so, but the hindrance of being born a woman is one I, unlike most men, do acknowledge. And thirdly, though by no means lastly in my mind, is that fact that you, like me, have chosen to lead a life that is divided into compartments. You must be many things to many people, and no one other than yourself knows the full truth. People who can do this are rare. And that you chose to do this is rarer still. If you question why I did not choose one of my fellows in my department I refer you to my first reason for choosing you.

I also, despite my training, confess to some affection for you. But have no fear, this will not descend into some mawkish love letter. If King and Country had required me to shorten your life I would have done so without hesitation, although with some regret. This is a significant admission for me, for in general I do not think much of my fellow men – or women. Perhaps what I enjoyed so much about you was you were always something of a puzzle. As I am too.

But that must suffice for our farewells. Here is your first task...

I read the task through three times. By the time I had begun my fourth reading my heart had slowed to a near normal rate. I could do this. It was not a dangerous task. It was certainly something I would not feel comfortable doing, and it would involve a great deal of lying on my part. The biggest stumbling block that I could see was that there was no way I could achieve this without Bertram's help, and yet within the task Fitzroy explicitly asked me to tell no one else of this adventure.

Convincing Hans and Richenda to allow me

39

some time away from the house now seemed like child's play considering what I now needed to plan.

Chapter Six

In which Bertram, as ever, causes problems – and before he has even arrived

I made what plans I could. I managed to liberate some of Richenda's older items of clothing. I simply rooted through her wardrobe when she was tending to Amy and removed a few articles that were by now far too small.

Richenda, if she thought anything about it at all, would assume that either her new lady's maid, a severe woman named Trevors with whom I had little interaction, had removed them to spare her embarrassment, or that they were away to be laundered.

Richenda's attitude to her wardrobe was for the most part thus: if she had worn items once she wanted something new and exciting. I had noticed that Trevors was excellent at re-trimming a dress so it looked quite different. There was also a distinct difference now between the outrageous concoctions Richenda wore around the estate and what she wore in society.

Despite her devotion to Richenda's wardrobe, however, Trevors avoided Amy as if she was some serious contagion.

My mother has always been horrified by my needlework, but I am competent enough. I spent the time awaiting Bertram's arrival – I had no doubt he would accept the invitation to a warm, friendly, and water-tight house with alacrity – stitching my costumes. I spent some time consulting the fashion magazines that Richenda regularly received, but were currently being left unread, so I could aim at the right styles. Personally, I am no great follower of fashion, preferring to wear something that suits me, and the only nod to fashion I tend towards is wearing the correct hem length. However, the woman I would impersonating would be far more fashionable than myself.

Hans did once intrude upon my solitary sewing waving a letter.

'I've got the best...' he began, and then took in my activity. I have learned that nothing looks so guilty as to hide something that has already been seen, so I attempted to brazen it out with a smile on my face.

'Yes?' I encouraged.

'Why are you sewing, Euphemia? We have a house seamstress.'

'She is busy with clothes for Amy. The poor child has almost nothing.'

'That is no excuse for her to neglect you,' said Hans sternly.

'No, she hasn't,' I responded quickly. 'I didn't even ask her.'

Hans' expression softened. 'Euphemia, you have the status of a lady of this house now. You have no need to tend to such menial tasks.'

41

As a companion I certainly did not have the status of a lady, as my mother pointed out repeatedly in her letters, but I knew Hans meant well.

'I shall go to her next time,' I promised. 'Now do tell me your news.'

'This is a letter from Sir Richard Stapleford,' said Hans, pulling a face. He disliked Richenda's twin almost as much as I did. 'He is sending Merry to us for the next six months. Which is extremely kind of him.'

'I am surprised he has interested himself in the matter. I wrote to Mrs Lewis.'

'That is because he is keen to make me aware that Amelia does not, despite our adoption of her, count as a legitimate heir.'

'Oh, Lord!' I said. 'He can't still think Richenda wants to own Stapleford Hall?' Although Richard has assumed control of the house as the eldest son, the terms of his father's will left the house to the first of his children to have a child.

'I have never discussed it with her,' said Hans. 'Honestly, what that wretched building represents to the three of them is quite beyond my understanding.'

'But this is such a beautiful estate!'

Hans smiled. 'I think so, but you know how strange the upbringing of the Stapleford children has been. I am sure the only consistent thing in their childhood was that house, and certainly their father thought more of the Hall than he ever did of them or either of his wives.'

Although raised as an English gentleman, on rare occasions Hans does display the European

42

blood within him. I made no answer to his extra-ordinary speech.

'But,' said Hans, 'further good news. Bertram will be with us within the week.' He paused and bit his lip. 'It seems he is bringing Rory McLeod with him. That won't be a problem for you, will it?'

'Rory?' I said blankly.

'It seems he did indeed resign from Stapleford Hall, and has been working as a butler at White Orchards. Bertram wants to bring him as his valet, but he ... he wrote to, er, check first.'

I felt myself blushing and focussed my attention on the sewing in my lap.

'As you say, Hans, I now have the status of a lady resident in your house, and I am sure it is no concern of mine whatsoever which servants your guests choose to bring with them.'

Hans' uncertainty radiated out from his person. I kept my head down and said nothing further. After a longer pause than either of us was comfortable with Hans said, 'Of course.' I heard him close the door softly behind him.

Damn, but this was going to make things more difficult! Yet by the time Bertram arrived I was all in readiness. Merry should arrive shortly, and as soon as she did I intended to make my escape. I was sure she would be distraction enough for Richenda. So Bertram had barely had his luggage unloaded when I accosted him in the lobby.

'I will need to speak to you privately,' I said quietly. 'I think it might be wise to advise your valet not to unpack fully.'

Bertram's eyes bulged and he looked most

43

alarmed. Hans and Richenda then appeared, to welcome him, and I slipped into the background. I hoped I had alarmed Bertram enough that he would spend the rest of today and tonight in terrible and wild imaginings of what I might ask, so that when my favour was asked it would seem almost inconsequential in comparison.

Or at least this is what I optimistically thought. At dinner that night Bertram continued to glance at me in boggle-eyed alarm whenever he thought our hosts were not watching. I managed to remain completely quiet and demure during the meal, which I think everyone found slightly unsettling. Indeed, when we withdrew Richenda asked me if I was feeling quite well.

'I'm well,' I replied, pouring tea for us both while we waited for the gentlemen. 'I believe Merry will be with us shortly.'

'Thank goodness,' said Richenda. 'I am worn to a frazzle. I think Hans is right, we need to set up the nursery properly. After all one day I hope...'

She became acutely interested in spooning far too much sugar into her tea.

'Indeed,' I said. 'I am sure that day will arrive very soon. This is an excellent opportunity to get everything in readiness.'

Richenda gave me a shy smile. Richenda doing shy is a most unnatural sight. She is generally too big and brash to be anything other than robust, but as this moment she almost looked vulnerable.

'I must do my best by Hans,' she said. 'I owe him everything.' I thought I even saw a tear in the corner of her eye.

'You have married excellently,' I agreed.

44

'Though I doubt we will see the men again to-night.'

Richenda frowned. 'Yes, I expect they will get horrendously drunk. Aren't men terrible creatures?' she said without rancour and, despite our excellent dinner, reached for a macaroon. Everything was back to normal.

I enlightened Bertram of my favour the following morning. We were the first at breakfast so I took the opportunity then, as I found him sitting at the table sipping black coffee and picking half-heartedly at a piece of dry toast.

I rushed through my explanation.

'So you see we would only be away for a few days. We do not even need to stay in London. I will only require a few hours there and then we can move on to the countryside. I am sure it will be easy enough to find a respectable inn, but one where we need never be known.'

Bertram, clutched the sides of his head and groaned. Hans had obviously been extremely free with his cellar last night. 'I don't think I'm following all of this,' he said. 'Are we eloping?'

'Good gracious me, no.'

'I just wanted to be clear on that.'

Some devil on my shoulder prompted me to ask, 'Why don't you want to elope with me?'

'I don't need to elope with you,' said Bertram.

'You don't know my mother,' I said under my breath. She would consider Bertram far below me on the social scale. Though, he of course, has no idea of this.

'Socialist type, is she?' asked Bertram, who I

45

hadn't thought was listening. I decided to redirect the conversation.

'So will you do this for me?'

'No, of course not,' said Bertram. 'It would be highly improper.'

Richenda chose this moment to enter the breakfast room, so I could not continue the discussion. I contented myself with kicking Bertram, very hard, on the shin. He gave a muffled yelp, but Richenda was in full steam heading for the kippers, and noticed nothing.

Chapter Seven

In which I unscrupulously bend Bertram to my will

For the rest of the day, whenever he saw me in company Bertram made a pretence of limping. Whenever he found himself alone with me he shot out of the room at high speed. It was exceedingly tiresome. I knew I would bend him to my way of thinking. I had to. The only question was how.

In the end I decided I would have to begin my lying career with Bertram. I hated to do this, because although we had often fought in the past I had never lied to him. I had not told him about my background, it was true, but I had never lied and today I would have to start.

I bearded him in the smoking room. He was

46

sitting in one of the wing-backed chairs Hans favours, his eyes closed and a small cheroot between his lips. His feet were stretched out towards a blazing fire and there was an expression of bliss upon his face.

'Bertram,' I began in a reasonable tone. However the sound of my voice produced the most unexpected effect. Bertram leapt to his feet as if the chair had bitten his backside. For a moment I thought he had actually swallowed his cheroot. But fortunately he had merely dropped it. The edges of his jacket smouldered slightly and the next few minutes of his attention were taken with flinging the cheroot into the fire and attempting to ensure he did not go up in flames.

'Damn it, Euphemia,' he expounded once he was suitably extinguished. 'This room is meant to be safe from women!'

'Richenda comes in here all the time,' I countered.

'Poor Hans,' said Bertram with deep feeling. 'Allow me to further your education, Euphemia. Ladies do not enter smoking rooms.'

'This one does,' I said and sat down on a chair opposite him. 'You know you're going to agree to my plan in the end, so why all this hassle and pretence?'

Bertram adopted a mulish look. 'I could escape by returning to White Orchards.'

'Oh, is it above water again?'

Bertram threw me an evil look. 'It's really you I am thinking of. You cannot travel unchaperoned with a single man.'

'It's not that, or not entirely that,' I conceded.

47

'We have travelled alone before. That time we went on the train to the Lodge where all the Smiths waited for us.'

'I wasn't happy about that,' said Bertram, 'but we were doing our duty for King and Country.'

I gave him a long, low, level look.

Bertram's eyes widened. 'Oh no,' he said. 'Oh no, no, no.'

'I can't tell you anymore,' I said, quite truthfully. Bertram leapt neatly to the wrong conclusion.

'But, damn it, I've signed the Official Secrets Act too!'

'Ours not to reason why ... so will you help me?'

'Of course,' said Bertram. 'And don't tell me bloody Fitzroy isn't behind this pulling the strings.'

I realised then that Bertram would have no way of knowing the spy was dead, but even dead we were both still dancing to his tune.

We made our preparations to leave the following week. Bertram suggested I came up with the story of visiting an ailing aunt. I confess having avoided mentioning my family for so long I was not keen on using such a ruse, but I couldn't think of anything better. All my thoughts were caught up with what I must do once we reached London.

'We don't need to stay overnight in London,' I told Bertram in a snatched conversation in the gardens one evening. 'But I will need a place to change. Perhaps a hired room above a respectable tavern?'

'We will stay in a hotel of the best reputation,'

48

said Bertram. 'And on different floors.'

I frowned. 'Hans and Richenda pay me well, and I have few expenses save supporting my own family, but I do not think I could stretch to that.'

'I'll pay,' said Bertram gruffly.

'I cannot allow you to do that,' I protested. 'That really would be improper.'

'Nonsense, it will be the least improper episode of this whole debacle. If you refuse to allow me to protect our reputations in this manner I shall refuse to accompany you.'

I am equal to many things, but even I quailed at the thought of finding my way to London and on into the deepest country alone. I sensed an inflexibility in Bertram here. He had curved and bent and moulded his morals for me on various occasions, but even he eventually drew a line in the sand.

'Thank you,' I said humbly. 'But you realise we cannot use our real names?'

'Yes, dammit,' said Bertram. 'But at least I will know I am doing the proper thing.'

The morning of our departure coincided by accident with the day Merry was due to arrive. Richenda was suitably distracted and a small emergency in the stables had happily taken Hans out of the house. I got one of the maids to carry my small suitcase down to Bertram's automobile and reflected that the sooner I was away the better. Merry was going to be furious that on the day she arrived I stole her Merrit, who was Bertram's chauffeur, away.

I buttoned up my overcoat and checked the pins

49

securing my hat. I would be travelling inside the covered compartment, but I could not believe the windows would be secure enough to keep out the draughts when we travelled at the reckless top speeds of over twenty miles an hour that Bertram favoured.

Bertram had had the vehicle brought round to the front and was already inside. Stone handed me up into the carriage. I thanked him. He shut the door. The engine, which had already been purring, roared into life and we bumped our way along the drive.

It was unexpectedly warm in the carriage and within moments I decided to take off my hat. We would be travelling for several hours and it was clear my wide brim was already threatening Bertram's vision. Fortunately, I style my hair simply and do not have to retire to have my hair re-done the moment I remove my hat, unlike some women. I feel there are already enough daily costume changes forced on us women.

It took me a few moments and a little jiggling to remove the hat and pins safely. Both Bertram and I were a little breathless when it was done, but there was a look of relief on his face.

'I thought you were going to wear that dratted thing the whole way,' he said.

'It became clear as soon as I entered the carriage that doing so would have endangered the civility of our journey.'

'Indeed.'

I sat back in the seat. 'Ah, this is nice,' I said. 'I feel like I am travelling in style. How long do you think it will take Merry to forgive us for stealing away Merrit the day she arrives?'

'I didn't dare,' said Bertram. Then seeing my confusion he pointed at the chauffeur. Obviously the man did not turn round, but I knew him even by the back of his head. 'McLeod's been learning up on the estate. We are in safe hands.'

Words failed me. Of all the people Bertram could have brought on his expedition my (very jealous) ex-fiancé, who was as sharp as a tack and by whom I had never managed to pass a single ruse, was undoubtedly the very worst of all.

Eventually I managed to gasp, 'Oh, Bertram!'

He blinked at me in total ignorance. 'What's the matter now?' he said.

The conversation, which supposedly Rory could not hear because of the glass partition, continued for some time and became, at least on my part, rather animated. I am certain Rory could see us in the little side mirrors he used to look at the road behind, but his driving did not waver.

'Honestly, Euphemia, I'm not made of servants,' protested Bertram. 'I don't run the same kind of household as my brother, and certainly not as large as the Mullers'. I only have a small pool of people to call on.'

'Why on earth did you take Rory on in the first place?' I demanded. I knew I was being petty.

Bertram replied with dignity, 'Because he needed employment and I needed a butler.'

'But the two of you...' I trailed off, lost for words.

'On our adventure,' Bertram admitted, 'Rory and I were at odds. We have also been at odds over our feelings for you.'

I stiffened in shock. It was not like Bertram to

refer to these matters at all.

'But,' he continued, 'all those circumstances are in the past. I know McLeod to be an excellent, honest, and forthright fellow. I applaud his decision to take no more blood money from Richard. We have settled into a proper master and servant relationship.'

This, I thought, was something I'd have to see, and I said as much. Bertram then began to upbraid me about being a troublemaker. In the end I reached over to get my hat, plonked it onto my head, and tilted the brim so I could no longer see him. He humphed and huffed loudly, but I refused to be drawn. Even accusations of childishness did not stir me. I needed to think. Fitzroy had been clear about keeping my tasks secret, but I could see this was becoming more and more unlikely.

When we reached London, it was approaching the dinner hour. Despite the apparent luxury of the automobile I felt stiff and sore as I was handed down by the hotel doorman. Rory disappeared off to wherever the automobiles were put, and a sullen-faced Bertram and I made our way into the hotel.

'Did you make a reservation?' I asked.

Bertram gave me a wide-eyed look.

'Let me deal with this. You see to it that our baggage is fetched,' I said and without waiting I hurried to the desk.

'I am afraid my brother has overlooked making our reservations. I am wondering if you can help.'

The man behind the desk gave me an appraising look. 'I am in town to arrange settlement of some of my late husband's affairs,' I said. 'As you may appreciate we have all had a lot on our minds. I am looking for accommodation for my brother and myself for one night only. Our chauffeur will also need to be accommodated ... wherever you put chauffeurs. He is currently taking our automobile to your garage.'

It was the mention of the automobile that did it. For once I blessed Bertram's extravagance and determination to try all things new.

'We do have two rooms available,' said the hotel desk clerk, 'but they are not on the same floor.'

'Perfect,' I said.

'What name, ma'am?'

'Mrs Fitzroy and Mr Ellis,' I said. He was on the process of handing me the keys when Bertram appeared at my side. 'This kind man has found us rooms for the night, brother.'

'Will you be dining, ma'am? Sir?'

'Oh yes,' said Bertram.

I thanked the man and ushered Bertram away from the desk towards the bellboy who was waiting with our bags.

'You are Mr Ellis,' I whispered in his ear, 'and I am your widowed sister.' Bertram shot me a boggle-eyed look, but had the sense not to demand an explanation before the hotel staff.

Happily, at dinner we were beset with excellent service. The dining room was surprisingly busy and people were constantly passing our table. Bertram got no more opportunity than to shoot me the occasional question. I managed to keep the name I had signed in from him and also to tell him only that tomorrow morning at ten I had an

53

appointment I had arranged by letter. It was well within walking distance and I would be grateful if he would escort me to the street and then wait for me in a Lyons tearoom which I had discovered, through perusing a local directory, was nearby. Bertram's habit of starting his interrogatives by use of my name and, or, various polite expressions such as 'dash it' meant he took far too long to ask anything significant before someone came within earshot or offered us further courses. He was already annoyed and uncomfortable at having a false name thrust on him where he might, just might, meet someone he knew and eager not to attract attention.

I enjoyed an excellent meal. Bertram ate angrily and, as I pointed out, would doubtless have indigestion tonight. I advised him to send for some bicarbonate of soda before he retired. He did not thank me, instead contenting himself with glaring at me over the soup, frowning over the entrée, devouring the fish in the most sullen manner, and declining dessert. I had a large slice of lemon drizzle cake and ate every last crumb. Richenda would have been proud of me.

We retired with my naming the time I required to meet him in the foyer to set off my appointment. Bertram neither confirmed nor denied he would be there. Instead, he grunted goodnight. I told him he had the manners of a pig and tripped upstairs to my bedroom. I hoped I had angered him quite enough that he would not pry further into my schemes. Indeed, if I was lucky he might not speak to me at all before we got back to the Mullers' estate.

Chapter Eight

In which I am grateful for having a womanly figure

Bertram Stapleford is not a tall man, nor is he particularly broad in the shoulders, but he has the tenacity of a bulldog. Against the odds he was waiting for me in the lobby at the appointed hour. I thought the least said about our intended destination the better. I smiled at him very brightly, as if there had never been a cross word between us, took his arm, and marched out into the morning sunlight. I thought I had got it away with the deception. Bertram was silent for a while, but when he reached a place where the passers-by had lessened he finally spoke.

'I thought it would be better if we stayed in the hotel for another night. I know you have somewhere else you wish to visit and I felt it was better not to attempt too much in one day. I have little idea of what the roads will be like beyond London, but I suspect very bad.'

'Oh,' I said.

'The desk clerk was extremely helpful and not only accommodated us for tonight, but also the night on the way back to the Mullers. Though I do wonder if we should also break that journey, as it's so very long.'

'Possibly,' I said cautiously, 'I am unsure how

55

long the appointment after this will take. My information indicated it would be a three-to-four hour drive, or two hours if we took the train.'

'Do you want to take the train, Mrs Fitzroy?'

'Ah, the desk clerk told you the alias I used,' I said licking my suddenly dry lips. 'It was the first name that came into my head.'

'Of course it was,' said Bertram, achieving an admirable level of sarcasm. I felt myself blushing. But we were almost at the tearoom. Bertram let go of my arm and entered without a backward glance. From the set of his shoulders I knew he was not only angry with me, but hurt that I was intentionally keeping from him my mission. I wanted to tell him that it was not I that did not trust him, but Fitzroy, but if I was to keep to the letter of the will I was denied even this.

I walked up the steps of Black and Hunt, Merchant Bankers, and rang the discreet bell. I took out the flimsy veil I had stowed in my handbag and cast it over my hat and face. An individual with a countenance so devoid of expression he could have been related to Stone opened the door.

'Mrs Fitzroy,' he said. 'We have been expecting you.'

Of course they would have been. Fitzroy would have been nothing but efficient. I imagined there were a variety of events, people, signals, and ploys that he had arranged to be dispersed on his demise. I nodded to the man and stepped across the threshold.

Obviously, I have never been in a gentleman's club, but I suspect that Black and Hunt had been modelled on one. The lobby area was unusually large. Carpeted in thick red pile, bookshelves lined the walls and leather wing-backed chairs were scattered in small groups. Subtle oil paintings in overly ornate frames hung on the walls, and an enormous Grecian-style marble fireplace was filled with unlit logs.

Except for the two of us there was no one else present.

'If you will come this way,' said my escort, 'I will take you to Mr Grace. He is dealing with this aspect of the estate.'

I nodded again. My voice seemed locked away. This was the first time I had committed such a brash act of imposture and I was irrationally terrified that when I spoke I would give myself away.

'We are all very sorry for your loss.'

I stared at the man. This was not a sentiment I could respond to with only a nod. My tongue felt thick in my mouth.

'Of course. Thank you,' I managed to mumble in what I hoped was a grief-stricken tone. I was given a polite, but without doubt appraising look and then ushered into a small office. The door clicked shut behind me.

A gentleman of middle years, with a perfect parting in his oil-slicked hair and a suit so subtly elegant it fairly screamed 'I am a man of means', came forward to take my hand. Pale blue eyes gazed directly into mine. His hand was dry and slightly warm, his handshake of just the right pressure.

'On behalf of the bank may I express my heartfelt condolences,' said Mr Grace.

'You are very kind.'

'Our business will only take a moment. If you would care to be seated, Mrs Fitzroy, I must check your credentials. A formality, I assure you, but there is a great deal of money in this account and even under the most tragic of circumstances the formalities must be adhered to, must they not?'

'Of course,' I managed to say, but I was thinking wildly of how on earth could I prove myself to be someone I was most assuredly not. Could I say my passport had been lost at sea?

'Would you care for some refreshment? A small chilled glass of wine or a cup of china tea? Most ladies and gentleman find themselves in need of something in a situation such as yours, ma'am.'

I asked for a cup of tea, thinking it might buy me a little time. Mr Grace lifted the telephone on his desk and asked for it to be brought in.

'I am not sure what credentials you require,' I said nervously. 'No mention was made of bringing documents when the appointment was arranged.'

Mr Grace smiled. 'As you know, your husband had an abhorrence of documentation. He had, if you will excuse my saying so, a quite fantastical belief in how such things could be fraudulently manufactured.' He took a key from his waistcoat pocket and unlocked a drawer in his desk. He took out a file, relocked the desk, and again secreted the key away in his waistcoat. 'I think we will wait for tea and then we will conduct our business. I'm sure you will agree it will be much better if we are not disturbed.'

Though it is most unladylike to admit it, I could feel beads of sweat forming in the hollow of my spine. I took off my gloves and folded them on my lap. The action allowed me to take my gaze away from the man opposite. My heart was thumping. Fitzroy had done this day in and day out, and often in far more dangerous situations. I assumed the worst that would happen to me was I might end up at a police station. Fitzroy had always been only a few feet from danger and often death. I believe that is the way he liked to live. At this moment I would have given a lot to be back at the Muller estate, trying to deny Richenda a third slice of cake. That was the level of danger I enjoyed.

A slight knock the door opened and Mr Grace went over to receive the tea tray. I did not even turn round to see who delivered it. He set the tray on his desk.

'Would you care to be mother?' he asked.

'Certainly. Milk or lemon?'

Mr Grace smiled, flicked open his file and ticked off an item. 'Lemon, if you please,' he said. He set the cup I passed him down on his desk. 'Now if you could just complete this, please.' He passed two sheets of paper across to me and indicated a pen and ink stand on his desk. The first page was a list of persons, including an archbishop, a retired colonel, the spinster sister of an earl, a banker, a vicar who was also technically a baronet, and a lowly official from the Foreign Office. The other page was a blank dining table plan. I sighed.

'Who is holding this affair? Where is it? What time of day, is anything in particular being celebrated, and are any of the guests currently courting?' My question was met with a smile and I was given detailed answers that raised the complexity of the plan another level. It took me ten minutes to complete and hand back the plan.

'A competent butler could have completed this,' I remarked.

Mr Grace ran his eyes down the page. 'Perhaps, but there were some tricky elements and also some degree of choice. You have drawn the plan entirely as expected.'

I felt a little sting at that. 'Entirely as expected', not necessarily correctly. I bit my lip, so I did not blurt out an enquiry.

There followed a series of increasingly bizarre questions. There were more points on etiquette, particularly how it related to the clergy. Moral decision scenarios were posed where there simply was not a right or wrong answer, but I was still asked to proffer one. A few questions in Latin and a couple in Greek – the latter I was unable to answer, but this also appeared to be correct. I was even asked that if I had to murder someone, which out of poison, shooting, or stabbing I would choose! Of course, by now I was entering into the spirit of the thing and I asked a great many details about the situation before giving my final decision.

Finally, Mr Grace closed the file and sat back in his chair. 'Well done, Mrs Fitzroy. You have answered all but one question correctly.'

'Which one was that?' I asked, unable to help myself.

'I am afraid I cannot say,' said Mr Grace. 'But an allowance for two wrong answers was made by Mr Fitzroy.'

'And if I had made more than that?' I asked.

'Let us just say that Mr Fitzroy had certain

stringent plans in place should that have occurred.'

I shuddered. Mr Grace's smile widened. 'Exactly. I think we both know how diligent Mr Fitzroy was when it came to matters of security.'

I gave him a slight smile, but said nothing. For all I knew I was still being tested. I had no doubt that should I have failed to answer two or more questions in the way that had been predicted Mr Grace would have politely shown me from the bank, returned to his office, and placed a telephone call to a number Fitzroy would have left him. Mr Grace would only have passed on a message that a person had tried to obtain access to the account at a certain time, but I imagine he would have suspected the trail of action his communication would set in place. For all I knew *all* the OS officers used this banking establishment.

My legs were a little jelly-like as Mr Grace showed me to the vault. It struck me that this whole test revolved around Fitzroy predicting what I would answer to his questions. Not if I would get them right, rather that he knew me well enough to predict what I would say. This meant either that he knew me far better than I was comfortable with, or that he'd ensured I would have had to anticipate what he thought he knew about me. I was glad this thought had not occurred to me earlier. My head reeled with the implications. I could not help remembering that in his farewell letter to me, Fitzroy had described me as a puzzle. The man was, to my mind, a chancer, but on this occasion he had been playing fast and loose with my life. If he had not been dead I would have had strong words with him about it.

In the vault, a large, steel-caged affair with foot-thick doors that sprouted locking bars in all directions, Mr Grace, very properly, left me alone with a key. On one wall stood a bank of locked and numbered boxes. I located the one that matched my key and inserted it into the lock. Once the door was open there was a further, smaller box to pull out. It fitted so snugly into its place that I was forced to take off my gloves once more to pull it out. I took it over to a small table, presumably provided for this purpose, and opened the lid.

I do not know exactly what I had been expecting to find inside. I had imagined passports for various countries, foreign monies, perhaps even secret papers. What I found instead was a large amount of cash in various denominations of notes, none of them new. There was more money here than I would otherwise see in a lifetime. No bag, no note, no nothing – just bundle after bundle of cash.

There was nothing else for me to do but open the bag in which I carried my purse and a few personal items and attempt to stuff the lot inside. It did not fit. I realise I could have asked for a banker's bag, but that would have been akin to carrying a sign along the road that said, 'Rob me!' I cursed myself for not thinking of bringing something to take away whatever I found, and I cursed Fitzroy for not thinking of investing his wealth in something portable – like diamonds. Although if he had he would surely have sent me to a nefarious shop to exchange them for cash, so I supposed I should be grateful. In the end I was forced to utilise my underclothing as makeshift compartments.

And so it was I walked back alone to meet Bertram in that little café with an enormous fortune stuffed about my person.

Chapter Nine

In which my corsetry
draws unfortunate attention

When I arrived, Bertram was sitting with an untouched cheese scone in front of him, glaring very hard at a pretty little milk jug with forget-me-nots on it, as if he could curdle the milk. I sat down carefully.

'What's wrong with you?' he asked rudely.

I leaned over the table and said very softly, 'I forgot to take a large enough bag with me. I had to – er – do some makeshift stuffing.'

Bertram looked at me blankly. I directed my eyes to my corset. Bertram instantly turned a vivid shade of scarlet.

'Stop that!' I commanded. 'You will draw attention to us.'

'Good heavens, Euphemia, you mean you have got...'

'Yes,' I hissed. 'Yes. Now pay your bill and we can get out of here.'

Rather like a man sleepwalking, Bertram went up to the counter and paid his bill. I was glad he had not chosen to summon the waitress over, as glancing down I had detected the edge of a pound note poking out of my cleavage. I shuffled sideways (trust Bertram to choose a window seat), and with more difficulty than dignity managed to realign the stray bill. It both tickled and itched. Unfortunately Bertram arrived back at the table as I was completing my task and his face turned a deeper shade of scarlet.

'Fresh air,' I said quickly, 'before you have a heart attack.'

The cold air did do wonders for Bertram's complexion, but it caused other problems.

'I fear you will need to hail a taxi,' I said.

'I did not take you for such a frail creature,' said Bertram, trying to lighten the mood. 'It is no distance.'

'Things are ... shifting.'

For once Bertram caught on quickly. He hailed a cab most efficiently. However, when we reached our destination I insisted on paying the fare, and the place from which I produced the bill brought Bertram near to fainting.

Back in the safety of my room I disgorged the contents of my small bag and from about my person into a large carpet bag. I shoved this firmly under my bed. Then I locked the door and made my way down to the bar, where I knew Bertram was fortifying himself with brandy.

He spied me as I entered the bar. 'All ... er...' he began, and blushed again. Really, the man would have no blood left in his body at this rate.

'Stowed,' I completed. 'Yes. Now next I have to deliver the you-know-what to a vicarage in Abbots-on-Field. Do you wish to take the car or the train?'

'Expecting this, is he, this vicar?' asked Bertram.

'I very much doubt it,' I answered. 'And I need you on your honour to promise you will not disclose that you know the nature of my errand, nor where I have delivered the items in question. You were never meant to know even as much as you do.'

'Believe me,' said Bertram, draining his glass, 'the less I know about all this the better I will feel. Am I expected to meet the vicar?'

'No. I would prefer it if you waited with Rory in the automobile. Unless you want to take the train?'

'Take that amount of...'

I stood heavily on his foot. Bertram made an *ouch* noise that he turned into a cough.

'I mean, what you have, on the train? I would rather not.'

'And you are not to tell Rory anything!'

'Gracious, no,' said Bertram. 'He would, saving your presence, give me hell.'

'He is your servant,' I said shortly.

'Hmmm,' said Bertram. 'There are times when I wish someone would explain that to him.'

'Really, Bertram,' I said. 'Sometimes you are too soft.'

'Yes, like when I agree to accompany you on your mad schemes,' he snapped back.

Being now thoroughly irritated with one another, we agreed to meet by the automobile as quickly as Rory could bring it round to the front of the hotel.

Bertram arrived without any baggage as Rory was loading the last of my suitcases onto the rack.

'I thought we had decided it was close enough we did not need to stop in the country,' said Bertram bemused.

'I felt there was safety in a number of cases,' I said, glancing at Rory, who I had now established was in a not-speaking-to-me phase of our relationship.

Bertram looked blank, a far too frequent expression on his face of late, then his jaw dropped, 'Ah,' he said. 'Ah, um, I see. I had better send the porter for my bags.'

At this point Rory stopped being deaf and said, 'They're nae packed, Mr Stapleford. You didnae ask me to.'

I looked at Bertram exasperated. 'Wait here,' he said. 'Won't be a mo.'

With deep misgivings I climbed into the automobile. Bertram returned in less than fifteen minutes, so the disturbance we caused to traffic, parked where we were, was merely argumentative rather than disastrous. Rory saw off even the most foul-mouthed London carriage driver with a flow of incomprehensible, though obviously violent, Scotch invectives.

Bertram was followed by a young bellhop, who had an expression stating, 'It ain't my fault, honest!' on his face as he lugged a small case, out of which trailed two socks, a sleeve, and what I fear may have been a leg of some long johns. Triumphantly, Bertram bade him place the item on the rack.

'Packed it myself,' he said proudly.

'So I see,' said Rory under his breath.

One sock escaped entirely as the case was lifted up. I saw it, through the rear window, bowled along by the wind and skittering down the road making its bid for an escape into the wilds of London.

'Never liked the pattern,' said Bertram as he seated himself beside me.

'At least you will have one to remember it by,' I said.

Bertram gave me a slight smile. 'Funny girl. Don't know what Rory makes all the fuss about. Packing is quite easy stuff. You fling it all in and jump on the lid. When he's valeting it can take him a whole morning to pack for me.'

Expressionless, Rory started the automobile and climbed into the driver's seat. Bertram gave him directions and we headed off, leaving the metropolis behind us.

The day was fine and the roads currently good. Bertram was no longer scowling at me. Rory was shut away from us by a thick panel of glass. I began to enjoy the journey and watched the changing countryside around us with interest. Bertram leaned back in his seat and began to snore in a most ungentlemanly fashion. This signified, as nothing else could have done, that Bertram no longer had a romantic interest in me.

Chapter Ten

In which I have sherry with a vicar

In his instructions Fitzroy had told me only to ensure the vicar accepted the money and promised not to use it for the church roof or some other parish affair. He made it most clear this was intended for the vicar and his children. How I convinced the man to accept a sudden fortune from a complete stranger was entirely up to me.

I had made many plans by the time we turned into the vicarage drive, and discarded just as many. I bade Rory fetch me down the carpet bag and, struggling a little with the weight, I walked up to the vicarage and rang the bell. Bertram remained asleep and Rory knew he had to stay with the automobile. He knew nothing of my task, but the expression on his face betrayed a distinct disapproval for whatever I might be up to. I straightened my spine defiantly. It was nothing to do with him!

The vicarage was one of the larger sorts that could possibly once have been a dower house. It was a long, low house with many windows. It had a pleasant aspect down a short gravel drive. In front of the house was a large lawned area, perfect for holiday fetes, and under the windows sprouted flowerbeds with wonderful bursts of colour. I could see the curtains in the windows were a little frayed and shabby. I knew from my own upbringing that no matter how nice the house the church may give its ministry it does not give them a stipend large enough to generally keep that house intact. Certainly this house had a slightly shabby air. The window sills most definitely needed repainting and the varnish on the front door was blistering, but for all that it had an atmosphere of a happy place. Bees buzzed around the flower beds and somewhere a bird called. The sun had come out and was warm on my back. It was all very pleasant.

However, no one had come to open the front door. I rang again. From deep within the house a male voice called, 'Coming! Coming!'

The man who opened the front door was undoubtedly a widower. No wife in the kingdom would have permitted such hair at the dining table. It was white, long, and very wild. Surprisingly, he was clean-shaven as if while he remembered that cleanliness was next to godliness, and obviously bathed regularly, he had admitted defeat when it came to the top of his head. He looked for all the world as if someone had stuck a very woolly sheep on his head and forgotten to shear it for a few years. His face was wrinkled and I judged him to be well past his sixtieth year. He had a large and enormously hooked nose and deep blue eyes that twinkled.

'What a delight,' he said in the booming voice of a man used to speaking in church, 'A visitor!'

'Good afternoon,' I began, 'my name is Euphemia and I knew your ward, Eric.'

'Knew,' said the man, 'Ah, I think this is going

69

to be a conversation I need to have sitting down. Please follow me.'

I stood frozen for a moment before following him into the depths of the vicarage. It had never occurred to me that no one would have informed him of Fitzroy's death. Fitzroy had written in his letter that he had been known here as Eric, but other than that and the instructions on who and on what conditions the money must be given, he had been remarkably short on details. He had left me to accomplish the task any way I could, and considering the peculiarities of the case, I had decided to tackle it in a most un-Fitzroylike way and tell the truth as much as I could.

With quick, ranging steps, the priest led me into his study, and pulled a seat round to the side of his overflowing desk, so we were not opposing each other. Then he unearthed a decanter, and a couple of glasses from which he blew the dust. 'Sherry?' he asked. 'It's rather good. My son sent it down to me. I hate to think how he learned this was the one but ... I digress. Sherry?'

'Yes, please,' I said, knowing that unless I accepted he would not have one himself and by the shaking of his hands I could tell he needed one. When we each had a glass before us I said, 'I am so sorry. I assumed that someone would have contacted you about Eric.'

The vicar shook his head. 'No. No. He wasn't actually my ward, you see. He's my nephew. My oldest brother's son. I expect you've heard of him?' And he named a well-known and high-ranking aristocrat, who was a contemporary of my grandfather.

My knowledge must have shown on my face. 'Exactly,' said the vicar, 'rather a late marriage for my brother. He already had five children by his first wife. Two sons and three daughters. Eric, quite simply, was neither needed nor particularly wanted, except by his mother. Such a frail little thing, she died when he was seven.'

He gave a deep sigh. 'It was after that that he began spending holidays here rather than at the family home. No one there was interested in him, you see. His brothers and sisters were adults, or nearly so, by the time he was born. I expect they were also rather shocked that their father had sired another child at his age. All rather embarrassing. And then when Cecilia died...'

'I am sorry,' I said. The words seemed far too inadequate.

'Of course my wife was alive back then. Doted on the boy. We both did. Quite a scamp, but endearing with it. Had a vivid imagination. You know, he used to make up little stories about himself being this character called Fitzroy. *Fitz*, as you may know, meant one was born on the wrong side of the blanket in the olden days, and *roi* is French for king. He used to imagine he was the illegitimate son of the King, poor little mite. My brother and I argued violently over his lack of interest in the boy. Never really spoken since. Though he kept sending Eric to us. How did he die?'

'He was on board the *Titanic*,' I said. 'He died with heroism.' As he had not got off the ship himself, and I am sure that Fitzroy was more than capable of finding a way out of anything, I felt

71

certain that he had chosen to give his life so that more women and children could live. He would have been one of the ones calming things, restoring order. For all his coldness Fitzroy, I knew, could be passionate about doing the right thing.

'I would expect no less,' said his uncle. 'And I am deeply grateful that you have brought me this news personally. Er ... I don't suppose you were actually married to Eric, were you?' I noticed the involuntary glance towards my stomach and the hope that flickered in his eyes. 'Or even ... I must say, I am really rather broad-minded for a vicar.'

'I met Eric a few times,' I said. 'He was always a complete gentleman towards me. I believe he considered me a friend.' This was stretching a point, but considering his occupation I do not believe Fitzroy actually had friends in the normal sense of the word.

'Have you brought me his effects?' asked the vicar.

'Not exactly,' I said, and opened the carpet bag to reveal the stacks of banknotes inside.

'Good Lord,' exclaimed the vicar half rising from his seat, 'what *did* the poor boy get himself involved in?'

'Stocks and shares,' I said quickly, this being the only way I could think of that could raise such vast sums at a young age. 'He took great risks on the stock market, trading, and did rather well.'

'The risks I can well believe,' said the vicar. 'Well. Well. Good for you, Eric.'

'I am entrusted with bestowing this money on you, Vicar, but only if you are prepared to accept a number of conditions set out by Eric.' I took his letter from my bag and readied to read selected parts.

'How fascinating,' said the vicar. 'Why, I could repair the church roof with this lot.'

'Eric's first condition was that none of this money must be spent on church repairs,' I read.

The Vicar chuckled. 'He always was an irreligious little tyke.'

'He would like you to take a suitable portion to dowry your daughter.'

'Very kind. He was always fond of Susie.'

'He would also like you to send your son up to Oxford, or – and these are his words – Cambridge if you really must.'

The vicar felt in his pocket for a handkerchief and touched it to the corner of his eyes.

'He further states that as the church never paid you a tenth of what you were worth you are to take a significant portion for yourself to ensure you live out your old age in comfort and with plenty of good sherry.'

'Dear boy, but I really do not need much.'

'He is quite insistent that you are well looked after,' I said. 'He does add that if after all this you consider there to be monies left over, you can leave them to the charities of your choice in your will, provided both your children are faring well.'

'And how exactly does he expect to enforce – or for you to enforce his conditions?'

'He says that if you give me your word on these points there need be no further discussion.'

'That poor roof,' muttered the vicar. 'And there's the local orphanage. Oh dear! But ... he says I can distribute whatever is left after I die to whoever I choose?'

I nodded.

'Well, in that case, Euphemia, I give you my word that I will abide by Eric's conditions.'

I pushed the bag over to him. 'I believe this would have made Eric very happy. He writes in his letter to me that the vicarage was the only home he ever knew. He is eternally grateful to you and your family for the love and care you showed him.'

'More sherry?' asked the vicar. 'I would so like to toast our dear Eric.'

It was more than a couple of sherries later that I was able to tear myself away from the vicarage. I managed to avoid an invitation to dine, explaining my husband was waiting for me and this almost got Bertram included in the invitation. Fortunately I pled having to return to London by automobile. It seemed the vicar was extremely wary of such 'mechanical abnormalities', and wanted to allow me as much time as possible to return.

And so it was I clambered back into said abnormality with some difficulty. Rory had to leave his seat to help me in.

'You are plastered!' exclaimed Bertram.

'You should see the vicar,' I said, and fell fast asleep, my head in his lap.

Chapter Eleven

In which I suffer both a hangover
and a family revelation

I woke up in my room at the hotel. Bertram had obviously decided this was the best place to take me. Through my window I could see the beginning of dawn. I had slept right through the night.

The hotel still used gas lamps and mine had been left on low. I sat up. My head pounded. My eyes were dry and sore, and my throat felt as if I had been chewing a hedgehog. There was a glass of water by my bed. I drank it greedily, and then had to frantically scrabble for the chamber pot as I was copiously sick. I shoved it back under the bed. A slick of sweat had formed on my face, but I felt surprisingly better. I wriggled and loosened my corset. The relief was tremendous, for I had spent the night trussed up. I slipped back into a doze, silently blaming Fitzroy for everything.

I made it down to breakfast. Bertram was already at our table, tucking into bacon, poached eggs, and liver. I sat as far away from his plate as I could and ordered toast and fresh tea.

'You have a remarkably heavy head,' he said conversationally.

I silently nibbled a piece of toast.

'You slept all the way back from the country. You should have seen the looks McLeod got carrying you in through the lobby.'

I choked on some crumbs. 'You didn't!'

'No, we didn't,' said Bertram. 'We brought you in via the service elevator. In fact, I would say I went above and beyond the calls of friendship to get you here safely.' He attempted to give me a steely gaze over his eggs, though the beard severely limited the effect. I had to admit he had a point.

'I appreciate everything you have done for me, Bertram. I am in your debt.'

'And McLeod's.'

'He was only doing as you ordered,' I said, pouring us both more tea.

'That is not fair, Euphemia, and you know it.'

'I will thank him.' I swallowed a bit of dry toast with some difficulty. 'It really was not my fault.'

'I know the vicar got you drunk.'

'He did!' I protested. 'A vicar with a bottle of sherry is lethal!'

'What were you celebrating? Or is this how he treats all his guests?'

'Don't, Bertram. You know I can't.'

'I do not know anything of the sort. Can you at least assure me that you are not about to ask me to do something even more embarrassing or foolish?'

My thoughts turned to the envelopes upstairs. 'I have to go,' I said.

'I will extend our stay in the hotel, shall I?' asked Bertram. I put my napkin to my lips and bolted. Bertram started back in alarm, as I had intended.

My sickness had pushed all thoughts of the envelopes from my mind. I locked my bedroom door and with trembling fingers opened the letter

76

marked 'two'. Along with the letter there was a small package inside. I took out the letter.

My Dear Euphemia,

Many, many thanks for delivering my gift to my uncle. Unlike myself, he is a most deserving man, always thinking of others and rarely of himself to the extent that if my aunt had not reminded him to eat I think he would have perished long ago. But before we go any further, your reward...

Of course the only reward I can give you, that you would accept, is information and in my line of work nothing is as precious as information.

Your grandfather, the Earl of (we both know where) is desperate to reunite with your mother, your brother, and yourself. More than once he has asked me for information on you through various channels. As you will shortly come to understand, I operated a favours exchange scheme with many people of note. As you may know your grandmother died some five years ago. She was not a pleasant woman. Your grandfather was totally overwhelmed by her beauty. I believe many people at that time in society were overwhelmed by her, and your grandfather was generally accorded to be very lucky to have won her. Especially as it was well known she would have preferred a prince of the Royal blood. Needless to say, she was not happy with her lot as a countess. Having children greatly diminished her beauty, as it does with some women, and she resented them all for this. The boys, who were sent away for school and up to Oxford, entered easily into the society of their peers, but your mother, as was often the lot for girls, was left much at home in her mother's company.

77

Despite her small frame she was a girl of spirit and considerable attraction. She never equalled her mother's youthful beauty, but she was pretty enough to remind her own mother of what she had lost. To say that your grandmother was jealous of your mother is akin to saying that the Atlantic is a little wet.

Your grandfather was fond of all his children, but in keeping with the time spent his time hunting, shooting, fishing, visiting his clubs in London, and occasionally remembering to check that his agent was not running his estate into the ground. He never intervened with how his wife raised his children, and it is not that surprising that your mother, who was continually presented with a series of high-ranking, but elderly, suitors ran off with the handsome local vicar. The scandal was the talk of the country for quite some time.

Your grandmother never forgave her. She forbade your grandfather from having anything to do with his daughter or her family. Worse yet, on her deathbed, she extracted from your grandfather a promise to never again acknowledge his daughter or her children.

From this history you will perhaps have guessed your grandfather is not a man of great internal strength. In a man of lesser rank one might have called him henpecked or utterly under the thumb of his wife. In his defence I will only say that he is a man who has always taken any promise, from his marriage oath to his deathbed promise to his wife, very seriously. He is a man to whom honour is everything.

So there you have it. You now understand a lot more about your family background I am sure you can read even more between the lines. Your personal task, of course, is to find a way to bring your grandfather round to your mother's side. Your main advantage is

that the old man has been missing his daughter
desperately for years.
  And now on to your next task...

The letter fluttered from my fingers. Fitzroy had
assumed I knew the details of my mother's elopement. I had not. I knew her family had dis-
approved of her marriage, but the thought of my
mother running away with the local vicar was so
shocking as to render me near to hysteria. Worse
yet, the marriage had not proved to be particularly
happy. As I had grown up it had become clear to
me that while my parents did love each other, my
mother could never accustom herself to her new
lower status. If her parents had endorsed the
marriage I was suddenly sure that both Mother
and my beloved Papa would have had much happier lives. I felt a surge of fury towards my grandmother, and contempt for the weakness of my
grandfather. Sadness for my parents, who had
risked all for love, and not been able to live up to
their dreams overwhelmed me. I collapsed on my
bed and wept.

My weeping was not of the lady-like sort of
handkerchief dabbing, but the full-on howling,
blotchy-faced sort, which is why I did not hear
Bertram knock on my door. The first I knew of
his presence was being lifted up to sob into his
coat. His foul beard scratched the top of my head
and for once I did not care. I clung to him.

I am certain Bertram asked me many questions,
but I was too distressed to answer. Finally he gave
up and simply waited for me to cry myself out. It
took some time. Bertram did not comment, but I

quite ruined his jacket.

When I slowed to hiccoughs, Bertram took me by the shoulders and sat me back. I fumbled for my handkerchief and tried to mop up my face. I noticed my letter lay face down on the floor. The envelope was somewhere behind me on the bed.

'What is it you don't want me to see?' asked Bertram.

'Nothing,' I protested as I did my best to wiggle my posterior onto the envelope and slide the letter with my foot under the bed.

'I would not look at a private document un-invited,' said Bertram in a hurt tone. 'I do wish you would trust me.'

'Oh, Bertram, it's not that I do not trust you. I have been put on my honour not to reveal what I am doing.'

'Well, I would dashed well like to meet whoever has extracted this promise from you. It is obvious that whatever you have been asked to do is too demanding ... I mean, very demanding.'

I did not protest as I usually would at Bertram suggesting anything was beyond my capabilities. Without his help it would have been impossible for me to have even have completed the first task. Fitzroy must have meant me to, as he might have put it, 'utilise my contacts', but as he would have done keep everyone in the dark about what was actually occurring. This was not the way I like to do things.

'In fact,' continued Bertram, growing more animated, 'I would like to get the gentleman concerned alone in a room and explain exactly how one should treat a lady.'

I smiled. Bertram is the least likely man to resort to fisticuffs. I am fairly certain even my little brother, Joe, could defeat him. But I did not doubt his sentiment.

'I am afraid you cannot speak to him, Bertram. He is dead.'

'Oh, it is a will,' said Bertram, looking relieved. 'I believe people often do not give enough thought to how their instructions might be carried out. I suppose because they will not be around to have to resolve things.' He gave me a smile. 'But all we have to do, Euphemia, is contact the lawyer and say you require further assistance. Or even if the demands are too much that you find yourself unable to be an executor. You are not legally obliged to, you know.'

'I am afraid it is not that simple.'

'Black sheep of the family stuff, is it?'

'It is not a member of my family at all.'

'Well, good heavens, girl, why do you feel under such an obligation?' exploded Bertram. 'Were you in love with the fellow?'

'No,' I cried sharply, 'I most certainly was not.' I took a deep breath. 'No, I was not in love with this man, but he did on at least one occasion save my life.'

'But Rory is alive and well. At least he was last time I checked,' said Bertram, looking very confused. 'And I'm pretty sure you were in love with him.'

I ignored this last remark. 'Of course it is not Rory. He drove us to the vicarage, so it could not possibly be him. Unless you believe ghosts can drive.'

'Just as well you did not accept that invitation for us to dine,' said Bertram, momentarily distracted, 'turns out I had not packed any trousers. This luggage malarkey is far more complicated than I expected.'

'Indeed, dining at a vicarage without trousers would not be the done thing,' I said, and gave a little giggle.

'Now, it's all very well trying to put me off with talk about my trousers,' said Bertram.

'You mentioned trousers first,' I interrupted.

'But,' said Bertram loudly, speaking over me, 'who is this dead fellow that is causing you so much trouble? He's as pesky as...' He looked into my eyes. I dropped my gaze.

'Oh no, it cannot be. I would have thought that man was damn near indestructible.'

'I am afraid it is,' I said.

'Bloody Fitzroy,' said Bertram. 'Bloody, bloody, bloody Fitzroy. What on earth has he got you embroiled in? It'll all turn out to be some damn trick, you mark my words. I bet the bugger is not even actually dead!'

Chapter Twelve

In which Bertram displays a distressing opinion of my character

It took me quite some time to convince Bertram that Fitzroy was undeniably dead.

'I did not realise you were on the ship that picked up the *Titanic* survivors,' said Bertram. 'No wonder you are more ... feminine than usual. It must have been an emotionally scarring experience.'

I let this one pass only asking, 'Where did you think Amelia came from?'

'Oh, I knew she had been on the *Titanic*,' said Bertram. 'I just didn't know Hans and Richenda had got her fresh from the ship, as it were.'

'You make her sound like a fish,' I said in disgust.

'So will you show me this letter now?'

'I would feel uncomfortable doing so,' I said, desperately thinking on how I could play on Bertram's notion of honour. The last thing I wanted was for him to read about my family.

'But I've worked out who it is!' he protested.

'Indeed, you worked it out. I didn't tell you.'

'Yes, you did,' said Bertram, frowning.

'I only told you what you already knew,' I countered.

Bertram glowered at me and I feared another

lengthy argument. 'Can we compromise?' I said quickly. 'Perhaps if I could tell you what is in the letters without showing you? That would make me feel more comfortable.'

'On the condition you do not lie to me,' said Bertram.

As I had been lying to him for days I could hardly protest indignantly. Instead I agreed. I told him about the tasks, but I did not mention the rewards I had been promised.

'So what is the next task?' asked Bertram.

I picked up the letter. He rose and stood on the far side of the wall, so he could not possibly see. I curbed an impulse to smile at his seriousness.

Now, Euphemia, your next task should not tax you too onerously. I require you to go to the office of Sir Markham Linkwater, introduce yourself as my emissary, and ask to speak with the great man himself. I think you will find my name should give you entry, but if it does not, ask his secretary to send in a message that says you wish to speak to him about what occurred in the Winter Gardens in '01. That should suffice.

Inside this envelope you will find a further envelope. By all means open it and inspect the contents if you wish. However, you will find it contains photographic images of a senior civil servant cavorting al fresco and in a state of dishabille. Even for one used to amorous adventures, like myself, the sight is unseemly, and for your innocent virgin eyes it may well prove too much. If I was still alive I admit I would love to see the expression on your face seeing them – or even reading this.

Suffice it to say, Mr Linkwater has been under an

obligation to me since '01. I always promised that one day the proof of his indiscretion would be returned to him and this, or as near as dammit, is the day. I would ask you also to remind him that on receiving this he promised on his honour to complete one last task. I do not need to burden you with further details. I am convinced he will remember our conversation on the matter in question in perfect detail.

There, that shouldn't be too hard, should it? His office is at (here he gave a London address). *Get Bertram to take you up to town to see a show or some such thing and have some fun with this.*

Regards
F

'He wants me to return some blackmail material to a civil servant,' I said. The expression on Bertram's face was priceless. His jaw worked several times before he managed to speak.

'Good God, what a damned rascal that man was!' He came over to me and took one of my hands quite tenderly. 'I am sorry to say this to you about him. But clearly you cannot complete this task, no matter what feelings lay between you.'

It was then I realised Bertram had, with his unerring sense of misdirection, was not about to let go of his earlier wrong conclusion easily. He believed my tears upon his entrance, and perhaps even my more 'feminine' behaviour of late was due to my regard for Fitzroy. He believed I was grieving.

The easiest way to disabuse him of this notion would have been to show him the letter and reveal

85

the background to my family. I seriously considered this for a moment. If there was anyone I could trust with my family background it was Bertram. However, my mother's pride was such that she had only accepted that I might work if I used another name. If Fitzroy was right, and some day my grandfather and my mother were reunited, then perhaps it would all come out. But I suspected my mother would hope that to anyone that mattered in her eyes, that is, any member of the aristocracy, the story might never be told.

And in all honesty I could not face the emotional turmoil of answering the inevitable, and in all likelihood long, list of questions Bertram would ask. He would also doubtless feel I had deceived him and I would have to deal with his reaction. It was all far, far too much for me at present, so I did the only other thing I could think of that would disabuse Bertram of his notion.

I laughed.

He looked pleasingly nonplussed. 'My dear Bertram, while I would never wish any man dead I am not bereft that Fitzroy is gone. It is perhaps a little hard to believe that such a vibrant character is gone, but believe me, that is *all I* feel.'

'Of course. Of course,' said Bertram. 'The reality will not have sunk in yet.'

I was barely listening. 'To be honest, I do not think I wish anyone dead. Although I do wish some people were charged with their crimes and that might lead someone to be hanged. Do you think that's the same as wishing someone dead?'

'Let's go downstairs and get you a warm drink. I think it would do you good to be out of this room.

86

If it becomes known I have been alone with you in here for this long it could arouse suspicions.'

'I would hate to think that I would ever want to end another human being's life, but when it comes to someone who has committed murder and whom you help catch...' I trailed off. 'It all becomes very tricky, morally speaking.'

Bertram took me by the elbow and led me downstairs. Of course, I could no longer continue my previous discussion, so I merely commented on the elegance of the hangings in the hallway. This earned me an approving look from two elderly ladies, who were obviously long-term residents of the hotel, and a baffled look from Bertram.

He helped me very tenderly into my seat and ordered tea and crumpets. His face lit up when the order arrived and he began to thickly butter his crumpet. 'I take it this was comfort food at school?' I asked.

Bertram nodded and said something through his chewing. I only got the words 'study' and 'toasting fags'. Boys' schools have always been a mystery to me and I thought it better to leave it that way.

'So,' I said, 'how long shall I extend our booking at the hotel? Do you know this London address.' I recited the one mentioned in the letter. Bertram paled slightly.

'That's where your man is? He must be someone very important. This really isn't something for you to do.'

'For reasons I have explained to you,' I said, trying to keep my temper in check, 'I cannot pass

87

this task onto anyone else.'

'No, I do see that,' said Bertram, 'even if I think Fitzroy is being a damned rotter, I do understand how you feel honour-bound to keep this as secret as possible. But you still cannot go.'

'Then what precisely are you suggesting?' I asked acerbically.

'Oh, that's simple,' said Bertram, spraying crumbs across the table and dropping melted butter down his shirtfront. 'I'll go.'

Chapter Thirteen

In which Bertram takes charge but ends up in his pudding

It was, of course, a very bad idea for more reasons than I could easily enumerate in one single afternoon, but it was also extremely difficult for me to refuse Bertram's idea. In fact he made it impossible for me to do so. With great misgiving, I let him have his way. I gave him the enclosed sealed envelope and he went up to his room to change. I sat toying with my crumpet and trying to push the idea of disaster from my mind.

A little over an hour later, when I had moved from the dining room to one of the day lounges, Bertram made his reappearance. He looked discreetly dapper and there was an air of gentleman's toilet water that followed in his wake.

'You look very smart.'

'Tell me you did not look inside that envelope,' he said, his colour rising.

'It was sealed. Did you look?'

Bertram placed a finger under his collar and pulled. 'I felt I needed to know what I was getting into. Damned if I know how I will look that man in the face now. How did Fitzroy get those pictures?'

'He said they were "al fresco",' I said. 'Doubtless he was continuing his normal stock in trade and spying.'

'You mean he was watching while they...' he coughed hurriedly. His colour was now heading into puce.

'It's what spies do, isn't it? Watch people in private moments when they think they are alone.'

'But protecting the security of the nation and all that,' protested Bertram.

'I expect Fitzroy felt it was often too long to go through the correct channels, so he set up a sort of short cut with someone who would have his finger on the pulse of things.'

'You sound as if you approve!' exclaimed Bertram.

I shook my head. 'Oh, no – though I can appreciate the tidiness of it.'

Bertram regarded me much as if I had grown two heads. 'That damned man had too much influence over you.'

A retort rose quickly within me, but really it was better if this whole situation was got over and done with. There were more envelopes yet to be opened. 'Shouldn't you be leaving to catch this man in his office?' I asked.

'Yes,' said Bertram shortly. He formally doffed his hat to me and left. From the lounge window I watched him walking stiffly down the road. I wondered if his gait was due to his disapproval of the task, or simply the result of eating too many buttered crumpets. If the latter, I could only hope his trousers did not split at an inopportune moment.

I did not expect Bertram to return quickly. I had little knowledge of the locale, but I suspected he would have had to have hailed a taxi. I certainly did not expect him back much before dinner time. As such I spent the rest of the day lounging around the hotel and attempting to appear a lady of leisure. I read the periodicals on offer in the reading room. I gazed out of the window at the passing pedestrians. I tried to read a novel – the most pointless of pursuits. I considered visiting Rory or even summoning him to attend me in the hotel, but I suspected both options would cause outrage both to the hotel guests and the man in question. Finally I could bear it no longer and decided to await him in the lobby.

I had begun fretting so badly over what Bertram may have done that I was in danger of wearing a ridge in the lobby carpet. One of the bell boys had also begun to eye me in the most impudent way, when Bertram erupted back into the hotel.

The doors flew open in front him. He had not waited for the doorman to do his job, but had thrown them wide himself. He stalked into the middle of the lobby. His hat was missing. His tie was loosened and his eyes were glittering: with anger? Excitement? I could not tell. I only knew he had worked himself into a passion. I concluded the meeting had not gone well.

I managed to get Bertram into a private dining chamber before he let loose. Not a moment after I had closed the door, he blurted out, 'Damn man challenged me to a duel!' At this point the waiter, one I had not previously seen, joined us, requested we be seated, laid napkins on our laps and presented us with menus. I thought for one moment that Bertram was going to strike him. The waiter was certainly one of the braver members of the hotel staff, because despite Bertram's glowering aspect he merely retreated to the corner and awaited our instructions. Seeing no other option than to bodily remove him Bertram flung down his menu and instructed he would have 'whatever the chef decided'. I ordered quickly, choosing some of the plainer dishes. I have never felt more like skipping a fish course in my life, but some proprieties have to be observed or we would regress to the level of the jungle.

The waiter finally left us, but not before several backward glances. I suppose Bertram *was* a little dishevelled, but it hardly warranted such suspicion. As soon as the door closed behind him I asked, 'Did you fight a duel?'

'Good God, no!' snapped Bertram. 'Nobody does that sort of thing nowadays. But I will own things were a bit dicey there for a bit. Blighter thought I was Fitzroy! Seems they'd never actually met.'

'Of course! He would have been careful to protect his identity. I should have thought of that.'

'It would have been a ruddy sight more helpful if

91

you had,' said Bertram, savaging a bread roll with his fingers. 'Mind you, once we'd established I wasn't him and that neither of us had liked him a lot we got on like a house on fire. Keeps a devilish fine brandy!' At which point he hiccoughed loudly.

'Are you inebriated?' I asked indignantly.

'For God's sake, woman, you're not my wife,' spat Bertram at which moment the waiter entered with our soup. As he set mine before me I could see little ripples going across the surface. The man was obviously shaken; literally.

'I am afraid Mr Ellis has had a difficult afternoon,' I said to him. Both the waiter and Bertram gave me an odd look.

When he had left Bertram said, 'Dammit, Euphemia, did no one ever tell you one never apologises to servants. It only makes them drop their standards of service.'

'I have been a servant,' I said with dignity.

'Then you will know what I mean,' said Berram grumpily.

'So what did happen?'

'Drink your soup!' commanded Bertram. 'That damn waiter will be back any minute. He obviously got hold of the wrong end of the stick.'

'But I want to know what happened!' I objected. 'This was my task.'

'I'll tell you over your steak. That will be the longest course, they'll leave us alone.'

I had no idea what he was talking about, but Bertram can be as stubborn as a mule with a sore head when he puts his mind to it, so I did my best to contain myself in patience. Though I fear I may have hurried the waiter along a little.

The chef had chosen to give Bertram steak too, and over this he finally let me know what had happened. There was little to tell. Apart from the case of mistaken identity, which had been patched up over the best part of a bottle of brandy and some dismembering of the deceased personality, it had, according to Bertram, gone swimmingly well. 'Hate to think what would have happened if you had gone,' he said in a self-congratulatory way.

'Did he not react to the fact you had seen the – er – evidence?'

'I resealed the envelope. Told him I wouldn't have dreamed of opening the damned thing.' He took another swig from his wineglass. 'Really, I don't think the man himself could have done it better.'

'I suppose, then, that after we finish I must go and open the next envelope,' I said. 'I wonder what it will contain?'

'So far you have had to give money to a vicar and return some blackmail material. I think we can be assured that whatever is going to happen next will be even more exciting,' said Bertram. 'And when I say exciting, I mean, of course, damned inconvenient.'

'You are swearing a great deal this evening, Bertram.'

Bertram gave me a bleary look that spoke of the volumes of brandy and wine he had consumed. 'At least I am not considered to be a lady of the night by the waiter,' he said.

'What? Oh, that wretched bellboy! He was staring so rudely at me!'

'While you were pacing up and down waiting

93

for me, who you quickly thrust into a private room…'

'Oh, good heavens! But the staff know me!' I protested.

'Big hotel. Lots of staff,' said Bertram, who was now carefully measuring out his speech in a way I found most alarming. His head was also nodding over his plate. It finally collided with his rice pudding and if I had not grabbed him by the scruff of the neck I think he might well have ended his career right there and then. Considering my family background I was not prepared to let someone else die at a dining table if I could prevent it. I hauled him backward, so he was half-slumped over his seat and dangled just a little onto the floor.

When the waiter returned I gave him Bertram's room number and told him to add a discretionary amount to his bill for the staff's trouble. I then announced that I would have my coffee in my room, and emphasised that I was a resident, whatever the rude imaginings of a young bell boy.

On reflection I too must have slightly over indulged in the wine, because normally I would have followed my mother's precept of never explaining. As it was, I realised when I was seated in my own chamber that I might have been somewhat rude.

'Pah! Serves him right!' I said loudly, and unfortunately at the same moment as my coffee was delivered. I could only conclude that both Bertram and myself would be providing much of the discussion in the staff rooms today.

I poured myself a cup of coffee and fetched the next envelope. I felt it with my fingers. There did not seem to be any enclosures but paper. I had half feared I might find tickets to the United States of America inside. After all, that was where he had been headed, and who knew what business he had over there. Perhaps it was where he kept Mrs Fitzroy and all the little Fitzroys.

The sun had set and the room grew dark. I laughed. I knew that whatever was contained within this letter it would not be about his domestic arrangements. There had been nothing domestic about Fitzroy.

What I could not have predicted was how the contents of this letter would plunge both Bertram and I into the deadliest peril we had ever encountered.

Chapter Fourteen

In which Fitzroy asks an awkward question

I did not open the envelope until the morning. This was not so much fortitude on my part, but that after two extremely emotional days I felt I deserved a good night's rest before I embarked on whatever Fitzroy had planned for me next.

Dearest Euphemia,

I rather feel that now you know so much more about me and my work I am entitled to address you as dearest. The happy side-effect of being dead is that you are no longer able to berate me. Though I admit I would have given much to see your face on opening the envelope containing those photographs. I am sure an English Country Rose like yourself, even when transplanted into the inferior soil of the Stapleford estate, could never have imagined that two men could get up to such things.

My employment has rather hardened me to such nefarious goings-on. I am constantly prepared for the low morals and behaviour of some of this country's greatest and so-called good, and I am rarely disappointed. People, I am afraid, Euphemia, are in general not very nice. They are driven by greed and self-interest, and the men at least are also driven by lust. I confess I am really never sure how much a part this plays in a woman's life, but then it is not generally a side she is allowed to show. Overall, as Richenda's suffragettes have tried to explain, and generally failed, women do not have an easy lot in life.

But I digress. It is so rare for me to have a captive audience, who will actually pay attention to my words.

Your information reward in this letter comes in two parts. Firstly, may I suggest you continue to resist the charms of Mr Rory McLeod. I detect within him a jealousy and latent sense of inferiority which would at best wreck your union and at worst endanger you. Take this from a man who knows more about the human psyche than is comfortable for any human being to know. Bertram Stapleford, on the other hand, is a brilliant man, who needs a guiding hand. Preferably yours. He will be spared the coming conflict due to his heart condition, but he will want to play his part. If the two of you present yourselves to my department on the declaration of war I am certain necessary, and indeed *vital, work will be passed to you. Finding the enemy within, the spies hiding within our homeland, will be a great, but secret, part of the war. I have already put your names in front of the necessary individuals. You will merely need to be prepared to stand up and be counted. I know you will always do your duty, but I firmly believe it will be the making of Bertram.*

My second piece of information relates to the activities of Richard Stapleford. Both my department and that of Mr Edward have regarded this man and his activities with grave misgivings for some time. However, for political reasons, or connections with the well-placed, whichever way you wish to look at it, the man has been protected. You and I both know he murdered his father and he is complicit, if not actively involved, in several more killings. The late Mrs Wilson, housekeeper to the late Lord Stapleford, Richard's father, was believed by a select few to once have been his mistress. He was known to have a penchant for chambermaids. How Mrs Wilson overcame, or lived with his advances long enough to become his housekeeper I frankly have no idea. By all accounts she was an embittered and friendless woman. But for whatever reason, he kept her, and unknown to him I have received information from a most reliable source that Mrs Wilson kept a series of diaries over the years she spent at Stapleford House. My hope is that they would be incriminating of both the late Stapleford and the current one. Until the end, my source assures me, Mrs Wilson knew the innermost secrets of the Stapleford household.

I should add here I do not think this was a reason for keeping her as housekeeper, or even alive, but rather the opposite. I can only imagine that the Staplefords were never aware of her activities as a diarist.

As she had no other home, or indeed relative, this means these incriminating papers remain at Stapleford House. I know you have no love for Richard Stapleford, so I entrust you with the task of locating this papers and bringing down Richard Stapleford once and for all.

I stopped reading. I had also been told of these diaries by Mrs Wilson herself. I had failed to find them when I had been living in the house. Was this my next task? I could not even see how I would begin. Would Bertram be willing to uncover the evidence that would send his brother to the noose? We had tried once before and failed in the most noisy and spectacular way. I gathered my courage and read on.

Do not concern yourself, Euphemia, this is not your next task. I offer it only as information for you to do with as you will. All the tasks I will present to you should easily be accomplished within a few months, if not weeks. I do not wish to draw attention to what you are doing for me and any long undertaking would certainly do that. Also I am aware I am already trespassing on your good nature to a large degree.

So this task may be your easiest. If you have seen me die – if you have been to my funeral, that has been conducted by a reputable funeral director. Then you will be able to complete this task without leaving the room.

However, if there are any questions over my death – not over who may have killed me, I imagine it will have been someone who was simply doing their duty, for another nation of course. Or it may be that I died in a natural accident – which would be disappointingly tame, and I would hope I knew nothing about it at the time.

But. If my body was not recovered. Or if it was unrecognisable-able. Or not identified by anyone you would consider trustworthy...

Would you mind thoroughly checking that I am actually dead?

Yours as ever,
F

I could only hope Bertram did not have a hangover this morning. I foresaw I would need all the help I could get with this request.

My first sight of Bertram at the breakfast table was not encouraging. His cravat was floppy. His hair hung in lank strands, and the eyes raised towards mine were distinctly bloodshot. He was attempting to decapitate a boiled egg with little success.

'Tell me,' he said in a roughened voice, 'tell me that we are finished and are now going home.'

I sat down and took the knife from him, sliced off the top of his egg, and passed it to him. Bertram regarded it solemnly.

'Neater than Nanny,' he muttered. He sighed. 'I guess we are not yet finished.'

'Because I helped you with your egg?'

'No lady is ever that nice to me unless she wants something. In the normal order of things you would be berating me for being drunk.'

I felt myself redden. 'I am hardly in a position to criticise after my escapade with the vicar.'

Bertram's pale face broke into a grin. 'That was rather funny. You are very giggly when you are drunk.'

My face absolutely flamed at this.

'Tell you what,' said Bertram, 'Let's keep these few days between us. I blame the ghoulish influence of Fitzroy. I won't mention any of this to Richenda if you won't.'

'I have no intention of doing so. If you recall I was not even meant to tell you what was going on.'

'And what is going on?' A rasher of bacon finally parted under some incessant sawing. Honestly, it was looking as if Bertram needed his whole breakfast cut up.

'Your co-ordination does suffer the next day, doesn't it?' I said putting off the moment as long as I could.

'Nope,' said Bertram. 'My eyesight. Everything's decidedly misty. Come on, fess up. What has does he want done now?'

'He wants us to check he is actually dead.'

'That shouldn't be too hard,' said Bertram brightening.

'Especially as I was the one who confirmed he was dead.' And I proceeded to tell Bertram what had occurred on the *Carpathia*.

'They made you check the dead?' asked Bertram, shocked.

'But although the *Carpathia* seemed full to bursting a great many lives were lost before we appeared at the scene. The *Titanic* was far beneath the waves by the time we arrived.'

'Did anyone know what had happened to him?'

'I was forbidden from asking about him by name. Besides, we don't even know what name he was travelling under.'

'Sounds like the chances are that he is dead.'

'Yes,' I said. 'I do not feel that I could have done more at the time with the conditions imposed on me.'

'You do not sound convinced,' said Bertram.

'Maybe, after seeing so many dead bodies, it is hard to accept someone is dead when you do not see their corpse.'

At this point the waiter who had approached silently dropped the toast rack and slices of bread spilled out across the table.

'Careful,' said Bertram.

'I am so sorry, sir,' said the waiter.

I smiled at him. I knew Bertram had been referring to me. 'Accidents happen,' I said.

'Thank you, ma'am,' said the waiter. 'I will bring you some fresh toast at once.'

Bertram and I talked determinedly about the weather until the toast was safely delivered.

'What do you want to do?' said Bertram. 'Interviewing all the survivors would be an impossible task.'

'I agree. But I do think there is something more I should be able to do.'

Bertram looked at me hopefully. I stared into my teacup for inspiration. 'I am not going diving,' said Bertram warningly.

I looked up and smiled at him. 'You are certainly thinking big,' I said. 'We need something smaller. Something simpler that we can check that would give us some reassurance if not absolute proof.'

'Like if he got on the ruddy boat in the first place,' said Bertram, spooning far too many mushrooms onto his plate.

I clapped my hands. Then looked down at the offending appendages in embarrassment. 'Yes, that is exactly what I mean.'

'So you want to go to the port?'

'Yes.'

'Wait a minute. Was his name was on the ship passenger list?'

'I want to speak to the man who gave him his ticket. I want to speak to someone who saw him boarding the ship.'

Bertram sighed. 'I suppose it's better than searching the seabed.'

'We have to try,' I said.

'You will not feel you have fulfilled your duty unless we do, will you?' said Bertram gloomily.

'I am not sure even this will satisfy me,' I said. 'But I cannot think of what else to do.'

'Well, I suppose with what happened to the *Titanic* people are more likely to remember helping the passengers, but still, Euphemia, you have to remember there were over a thousand people on board. It is possible no one noticed him particularly.'

I snorted. 'Not Fitzroy.'

'Even if he wanted not to be noticed?' said Bertram.

'I admit that would make things more difficult.'

'Perhaps we can find out who he was sharing a cabin with,' said Bertram. 'He might even have survived.'

'Unlikely. There were some men from First Class who survived, but I think the others were those who rowed the few boats that were launched. Most of those were members of the crew.' I shivered.

Bertram reached out and patted my hand. 'It was a terrible tragedy, but such things thankfully occur very rarely.'

'I heard a lot of the survivors' stories. I did not ask them, but it was as if in the moments after being rescued they had to tell someone. If was as if they could not keep the horror within them. As the days passed and we grew closer to land, so those rescued spoke less and less.'

'Perhaps they wished to leave as much of the tragedy as they could behind on the sea.'

I nodded. 'Unless they have no other option I think many of them will never again travel by sea.'

'I have never been on a liner,' said Bertram. 'And I must confess the idea is much less appealing now.'

'She left from Southampton. That is where we will need to go.'

'I shall ask the concierge for a recommendation and write ahead to acquire us rooms at a decent hotel. I fear we shall have to break the journey. Hopefully, the roads will be decent enough, but I do not think we should force ourselves into too fast a pace. I fear this journey will be an emotional one for you.'

He paused and drank deeply from his coffee cup. I remained silent.

'I mean because of your experience with the survivors,' he added.

'I know,' I said. 'I would like to put those days far behind me, but I see no other choice.'

'You wouldn't consider...' began Bertram.

'No,' I said.

Bertram heaved an enormous sigh. 'Thought not. I better go and tell McLeod we're in for more travelling. I don't know how much longer we can keep what is going on from him. I only hope he does not take it into that thick Scotch head of his that we are eloping, or worse, that I am taking advantage of you.'

'It is rather the other way around,' I said.

Bertram looked pained. 'Please, do not say anything like that in front of McLeod. It is liable to prove painful for me.'

Chapter Fifteen

In which Rory becomes a bit of a problem

The journey to Southampton was long. Bertram's automobile was doubtless an expensive one, but whether it was his vehicle, the general state of the kingdom's roads, or even Rory's driving, I found travelling an exhausting experience. This is a mystery to me, as one is doing nothing but sitting during the whole procedure and looking out of the window or talking in veiled terms to one's companion. Perhaps it is something to do with taking in more and more views of the world that tires the brain.

104

We broke the journey at a mediocre hotel. I did not enquire where we were, but merely tumbled into bed after a tasteless supper. Despite my exhaustion the lumpiness of the mattress disturbed my rest terribly. So it was when we finally reached Southampton the next day, I only wanted my supper and my bed.

It was late afternoon and Bertram was eager to go down to the shipping office and start enquiries. 'I should think we have a full hour or more before they close,' he said.

'I am sorry,' I said. 'I wish to bathe, eat, and get a decent night's sleep. Until I have these I will not be good for anything.'

Bertram pestered and pestered me until I finally told him he could start the initial enquiries without me. Little did I realise that in so doing I had opened myself up to a most unpleasant experience.

I had had my bath and was in that lazy, warmed state of being that comes only from being immersed in gloriously hot water. All the smuts from the journey were gone and my hair no longer held that peculiar metallic smell that is produced by the fumes of automobiles. I had dressed, for I was intending to go down to dinner. The food one is served in one's room is never the chef's best and I was very hungry. When there was a sharp knock on my door, and before I even had time to ask who it was, the door was flung open and an angry Scotch man strode into my room.

It only took one look at his face to see that Bertram's fears had been well founded. Rory must have learned Bertram had gone down to the ship-

105

ping office and decided we were planning to sail away together. I decided to tackle him head on.

'If we were going to elope we would hardly take you with us,' I said coldly.

Rory, who had obviously been prepared for many responses, had not included in his imaginations my cold dismissal of his thoughts before he had even spoken. He looked startled and more than a little confused.

'If you would be as good as to close the door before you begin berating me,' I said.

'That wouldnae be right,' he said. 'You and me in a hotel room alone.'

I marched over to the door and closed it. 'Well, you should really have thought of that before you came up here,' I snapped. 'I have no intention of letting the rest of the hotel guests and staff know my business.'

'And what is your business,' said Rory, trying to grab control of the situation.

'I am executing a will,' I said with as much ice in my voice as I could muster. I had already thought through what I might say when Rory challenged me, as I knew he would. If I could manage it, I would tell him as little as possible. This desire was partly inspired by Fitzroy's command that I keep the situation to myself and also because I knew full well that when Bertram and Rory worked side by side, rather than as master and servant, they were prone to come to loggerheads.

My determination survived less than ten minutes. Rory was relentless in his questions and, more importantly, he was between me and my dinner. His stance and expression made it very clear that, no matter I was now technically his social superior, there was no way I was getting out of this room until he had his answers. I could certainly not push past so strong and tall a man. I was also unsure what would happen if we laid hands on one another. I was tired and I knew I was emotionally vulnerable. It would be all too easy to lean on Rory, to even attempt to rekindle our relationship, for I was far from indifferent to him, but Fitzroy's warning echoed in my mind, and his very action of coming to me when he had no right to question anything I did showed a jealous turn of mind that any lady might shrink from.

I made one last attempt. I stamped my foot and said, 'Oh, for heaven's sake, Rory, I want my dinner.'

Unexpectedly, he laughed. 'All right, I believe you.'

'Why?' I asked suspiciously.

'Even you, Euphemia, are feminine enough not to have a hearty appetite on the brink of an elopement.'

'I am not sure I find your statement complimentary. Particularly the part about *even I* being feminine enough.'

'Oh, for heaven's sake,' said Rory. 'Ye've won.'

'Moreover,' I continued, still feeling decidedly ruffled, 'there would be no need for an elopement. Bertram can marry whoever he wishes as can I.'

Rory made a humph-ing butler noise. 'I suppose Richenda would welcome you as a sister with open eyes?'

'She would not have any say in the matter,' I

declared hotly.

'So you are going to marry yon wee mannie?'

'He is not wee!' I protested.

'He's guy shorter than me.'

'You are overly large,' I said with as much dignity as I could muster. Rory bristled visibly, but I knew this had nothing to do with my comment on his height.

'However,' I said holding up a hand, 'I have no intention now or ever of marrying Bertram. He is a dear and good friend, but nothing more.'

'Which is why the pair of yous are galumphing all over the place.'

'I never galumph!'

'Aye, well, whatever ye're doing. Making me drive you like I am some ... automation.'

'It is your job, Rory,' I said. 'If you do not like it then you should seek another situation.'

'So that's what ye want me to do, is it? Get out of your hair? Leave you to get up to goodness knows what! Well, I shan't do it!'

Never had Fitzroy's warning seemed so apt. Rory had no claim over me whatsoever, but here he was acting like a jealous husband.

'Rory,' I began carefully, but as I was framing how best to approach the situation the door burst open, and Bertram stormed in.

'It's no damn good, Euphemia,' he said, not noticing Rory who stood off to one side, 'I eventually bribed the man to see the passenger list. Over two thousand names, and me with no idea what name the blighter might have been travelling under. We don't even know what class he was travelling in. I tried to describe him, but he always was such a slippery, nondescript kind of fellow that I couldn't make anything of him.'

'Fitzroy,' said Rory, who is far from stupid. 'This is all about Fitzroy.'

Bertram started, strode into the middle of the room and turned on Rory. 'What's this fellow doing in here?' he demanded. 'I thought we were keeping this all on a strictly need to know.'

'He is preventing me from eloping with you.'

Bertram looked a little awed. He addressed Rory directly.

'Don't know I could keep Euphemia from doing anything she set her mind on. Don't know I'd dare.'

Rory frowned.

'Oh, for goodness sake, man,' said Bertram. 'You know her well enough to know she'd be a damn sight too annoying to elope with.'

I bridled at this, but some communication passed unseen between the pair of them and I saw Rory's shoulders drop. 'Aye, well, ye have a point,' he said. 'I mind ye told me about the time she...'

'Yes, yes,' said Bertram, flapping his hands frantically, 'not the time. Euphemia, you had better tell Rory what this is all about.'

'What did you tell him, Bertram?'

'Nothing important,' said Bertram, still flapping. 'Bring McLeod up to date. He might have some ideas about how we can progress, because I'm plum out of inspiration.'

I sighed and explained about Fitzroy's will. Again, I left out the part about my information rewards, but I stressed the letters had been deemed for my eyes only by Fitzroy and I intended to honour his wishes. Fortunately, this did not seem to bother Rory.

'What you need is a sketch of the man,' he said.

'Euphemia?' asked Bertram hopefully.

'Drawing is not one of my talents,' I said.

'But you're a female,' said Bertram. I ignored him.

'I can draw,' said Rory. 'If you will ask the staff to find some paper and charcoal I reckon I could make a fair image of him. I remember him well enough. Dislike can do that to memory,' he finished darkly.

'But where will they get such things?' I asked.

'That's not your problem,' said Rory. 'It's theirs.'

It took the staff a little time, but drawing materials were procured and were sent up with a pot of tea and the muffins I had ordered. I poured the tea while Bertram buttered. Rory took a small table over to the window for better light and began to draw.

Bertram and I fortified ourselves. In less time than it took for the pot to cool, and this may have been an incentive, Rory had produced the outline of a rough sketch. He came over to get his tea and passed Bertram the sketch.

'That's him, isn't it? I can fill in more details, but I need to know I've captured his likeness.'

Bertram nodded. 'It is really rather good, McLeod. Have you ever thought of becoming an artist?'

Rory gave him an incredulous look. 'I prefer a living wage,' he said, and bit into a muffin. 'Ah, this is good,' he said through a mouthful of crumbs. 'You have no idea how badly I eat while you're dining a la carte.'

'I presumed you went out to the local public house,' said Bertram.

'Aye,' said Rory darkly.

Bertram muttered about having to do something about this, but seeing as he could hardly invite his chauffeur to dine with him, I attempted to head the conversation in another direction.

'What shall we do next?'

Bertram nodded his head at Rory. 'I'll take his sketch back down to the shipping office tomorrow and show it around.'

'Do you think it's wise to draw attention to yerself when it's this mannie in question? We dinnae ken if he still has enemies around.'

'Don't be silly,' said Bertram. 'He's dead and who would be interested in us?'

I felt the pit of my stomach drop. I was beginning to have a really bad feeling about this.

Chapter Sixteen

In which the tea is particularly thick and Rory gets restless

The next morning it was finally agreed, after a determined, but hushed argument round by the hotel garages, that Bertram would take the sketch. However, Rory and I would also be present, though separate, down at the docks in case things took a turn for the unusual.

Rory drove us down and parked discreetly two streets away from the dockside. 'I don't know what all this fuss is about,' moaned Bertram. 'The man's dead for heaven's sake.'

'Do you not remember what he did for a living?' asked Rory. 'The man probably had more enemies than your sister has eaten cakes.'

'I say,' said Bertram, 'that is not a nice thing to say about my sister.'

'I take it you consider yourself one of the team once more rather than a chauffeur,' I said.

'Oh, Lord,' said Bertram. 'I'm off before he starts calling me Bertram again. You are too much, man.' And so saying he set off at brisk pace towards the docks.

'He has a point,' I said. 'You are rude to him.'

'And you've always been the perfect servant!'

'No,' I admitted, 'but I am not rude.'

'If he doesn't like it he can sack me,' said Rory scowling.

'You know Bertram would never turn anyone off into destitution, because that is where you would be without employment, Rory.'

'I have more than one permanent offer of work elsewhere,' sniffed Rory.

'So why do you stay?' I demanded crossly.

'Come on,' said Rory. 'Bertram is disappearing over the horizon. Take my arm and we can look like we are strolling down to look at the liners.'

'Will there be any in?' I asked, diverted. 'I hear the ones that sail from here are much larger than the ones I have been on.'

Rory's scowl deepened. 'I forgot ye had been sailing.'

112

'It is not something I would care to repeat,' I said, my mind returning at once to the fateful night of April 14th.

Rory did not answer, but set a cracking pace.

'Careful, we do not want to catch him up,' I warned. Indeed, we arrived down by the dockside to see Bertram determinedly march up to and into the shipping office, a low white building that stood on its own near the dockyard. I could tell by his gait he was in the mood for a fight.

I sighed. I did not expect it to go well.

'Aye,' said Rory, following my gaze, 'I think Bertram would do well to remember you catch more flies with honey.'

'Well, it's too late to tell him now. Shall we take a turn around the public areas, as if we are admiring the ships?'

Rory looked down at me. 'You are looking a bit too genteel for my liking.'

'This is an old dress. I put it on purposefully.'

'You've been living among the toffs long enough you've forgotten what it's like to be poor.'

'I shall try and speak common,' I said, trying and failing to affect an accent.

Rory laughed. 'I recommend you keep your mouth shut unless it's to ooh and ahh at the ships. Remember, the likes of us can't afford to go on these luxury liners.'

We wandered along the dockside. It was surprisingly busy. No passengers were currently boarding, but there were three large vessels in dock that were obviously being resupplied. A row of smart motorised automobiles with names of well-known shops emblazoned on their sides stood alongside the more traditional horses and carts that were delivering simpler fare. Rory cast a knowledgeable eye over the greengrocer's supplier.

'Looks like only the best for the First Class passengers. That ship must be getting ready to leave soon. Some of the items being carried on board will not last long.'

'I do not see any passengers,' I said.

'I imagine they keep the loading of supplies and the loading of passengers as separate as possible. The last thing any captain wants is stowaways creeping on board. With these big ocean-going liners there is not much that can be done if someone is found far enough out to sea.'

'The *Titanic* docked at Cherbourg and Queenstown in Ireland before heading off to New York. I looked it up in the newspaper room in the hotel. They keep papers going back for quite some time.'

Rory groaned, 'So our man could have got off at either of those two places.'

'I am unclear if passengers disembarked there,' I said. 'From what I read I thought they were merely taking on provisions.'

'As if that would stop someone like Fitzroy jumping ship if he wanted to.'

'I see your point of view,' I said. 'This is hopeless, isn't it?'

And as if in harmony with my mood the skies suddenly opened and rain poured down. We were both in hats and coats, but the sudden deluge was extreme.

'This way!'

Rory took me by the hand and pulled me into what can only loosely be described as a tearoom.

The windows were thick with mist from the huge boiling metal geysers which were used for supplying what turned out to be the thickest tea I have ever tasted. Small wipe-down tables were packed close together. There were no chairs, only benches. The air was rich with the spicy language of the dockers, who sat in rough, working clothes hunched over enormous cups of tea. If Richard Stapleford had not been so free in his language I think I would have fainted at some of the expressions I heard. As it was I merely felt my ears glow a bit.

Rory deposited me at a secluded table and went to buy us some tea. This was not the sort of place where orders were taken at the table. In fact I am sure Bertram would rather have been soaked to the skin than enter such a lower-class establishment. I rubbed a patch clear on the window with my glove and looked out. The rain appeared to be coming down in sheets. I could just make out the shipping office. There was no sign of Bertram.

Rory came back with two large mugs and a plate with thickly sliced bread and dripping. The bread and dripping tasted good on such a cold and wet day and I tucked in eagerly. However, after one cautious sip of the tea, I decided I would rather like to keep the enamel on my teeth, and used the mug only to warm my hands.

'It is a bit much even for me,' said Rory.

'Mrs Deighton used to say strong tea put hairs on your chest,' I recalled. 'I never quite saw how that was meant to be an inducement for me to drink it.'

Rory smiled, a genuine smile. It changed his

115

whole face and lit up those glorious green eyes of his. 'If that's the case I think this is designed to make you grow fur,' he said.

'I suppose that might be useful if you are working on the docks in all weathers,' I said.

Rory grunted and took another glug at his tea. I looked around me. I was beginning to feel a little more comfortable. Now we were settled with food and no one had asked us our business, I felt I could raise my eyes from the table and take stock of the room.

As well as the dockers, who were obviously in for a warm between shifts, I saw a few small huddled groups of men, women, and children. They each had a battered suitcase or a bundle at their feet.

'Passengers?' I asked Rory.

'Perhaps, third class I imagine. Or it could be people waiting hoping someone has a ticket or two they can't use.'

'Does that happen often?'

'I don't know,' said Rory. 'But they are some folk who are desperate to try and start a new life abroad. I wouldnae be surprised if you found some of the poorer types came down here on the off chance they could get a ticket or maybe even find someone who would let them work passage. These big liners need as many crew as they have passengers, and some of them, like the engine stokers and cleaners, don't exactly need to be skilled. Willing is more important.'

'Some people do manage to stow away.'

'I think not often,' said Rory, 'but yes, the ships are so big, and there are so many people milling around when they are being loaded, it would be all too easy to get aboard. It would be hiding until out at sea that would be the hard part.'

'How would you get on board?' I asked curiously.

'Oh, I'd pick up a sack of rice or something going to the kitchens. Follow the other loaders. Deliver the sack, and then sneak off to hide myself. The problem being I'd only have what had in my pockets to bring with me. I could hardly carry a suitcase on too. I'd have to be very desperate to do it, but there are folks starving, and when you're that poor I reckon you might not think you have a lot to lose. As long as you don't steal anything, if you're caught in the dock the worst thing that is going to happen to you is you get a warm night in a police cell.'

I reflected unhappily that, much as I might despise Richard Stapleford, if he had not given me my original employment, my mother, brother, and I would have faced destitution.

'Och, don't look so serious, lass. The tea's not that bad. Drink up. It's time we went and met Bertram at his rendezvous. I wonder how badly it's gone.'

I opted to leave the better part of my tea. The rain had eased to a fine drizzle. Rory and I made our way back to one of the official viewing areas and waited, under an awning, for him to arrive. We moved back towards the shadows so as not to draw attention to ourselves.

It was cold enough to make me shiver. I began to regret not drinking the warming tea. 'Where is he?' I muttered.

Rory took out a small pocket watch. 'He's late,' he said. 'Maybe he has had more success than we thought.'

I rubbed my hands together to try and keep warm. Time passed. Bertram did not appear. Rory checked his pocket watch again.

'I think we may have a problem,' he said.

Chapter Seventeen

In which Bertram proves to be a problem

'Even Bertram cannot have got into trouble in an office,' I said.

'It is what he did on the way there or back that worries me,' said Rory. 'I think it would be best if you stayed here. I will go to the office and ask after him.'

'I agree,' I replied. Rory's eyebrows shot up in surprise. 'I see reason in keeping sightings of us separate. It makes us harder to trace. That is if we are presuming something nefarious has gone on in or around the office.'

Rory nodded. 'Let us hope Bertram has simply forgotten where we were meant to meet. I think you should go back to the automobile.'

I shook my head. 'No, I am going to find a vantage spot where I can watch you enter the shipping office.'

'And see if anyone escorts me out?'

'Exactly.'

118

'Please stay out of sight,' said Rory. 'If I do not return you will need to summon a constable.' He frowned. 'I mean that, Euphemia. No trying to come to the rescue. It would only end up with us all in trouble.'

I smiled in agreement. In truth, I knew I would determine what to do depending on the situation that presented itself. Rory knows me very well and he reiterated his point several times.

'You are wasting time,' I said. 'Bertram could be in real trouble. You know how weak his heart is.'

'Dammit,' muttered Rory. 'Damn Fitzroy.' And he strode off without a backward glance.

It was with some nervousness that I watched the office door. However, after a few minutes Rory came back out. He nodded with his head and I moved off in the direction he had indicated. We met up out of the sight of the office windows.

'They claim he was never there,' he said.

'But that's ridiculous,' I said. 'We saw him go in.'

'Short of hauling the clerk over the counter and threatening him there was nothing I could do. He flatly denied it.'

I made a noise of annoyance.

'I am not Fitzroy, Euphemia. I am not in the habit of physically assaulting people.'

'But Bertram's life may be in danger.'

'Indeed. I suggest we summon a constable,' said Rory seriously.

'Why?' I asked.

'To help us,' said Rory slowing his words as if speaking to an idiot.

'And we shall say your master, who I have been travelling with alone, and to whom I am no relation, has entered the shipping office and disappeared? Despite what the clerk there thinks?'

'Yes.'

'Do you think that there is even of the vaguest chance of us being thought reliable, decent citizens? Let alone our contrary and unusual story being believed?'

'You think they are more likely to arrest us for murdering him? That we are intending to run off with one another?'

'Something like that. Though admittedly we would have to be very stupid to draw attention to his disappearance.'

'Or very cocky,' said Rory.

'At least you see my point.'

'Yes, I shall have to investigate myself.'

'Even if we manage to convince the police of our pure intent it will take too much time ... wait, what did you say? You cannot go off alone. You will be captured.'

'Thank you for your confidence in me,' said Rory, coldly. 'I am neither as naïve nor as trusting as Bertram.'

'Look, let us think about this for a moment. Whatever happened to Bertram I doubt they could have risked letting him leave by the front door when they were going to deny he had ever been there.'

Rory nodded. 'There must be another exit.'

'I am sure we could take another turn around the docks without arousing too much suspicion. The rain has stopped and we might even be lucky enough to see some tracks.'

Reluctantly, after some more persuasion including suggesting to Rory I might not be safe alone, I managed to convince him that we should both check. The building was small enough for us to perambulate around in a few minutes. There were two doors at the front and one at the back. Bertram had obviously been taken from the rear.

We retreated to the tearoom once more. Rory got us both tea, but also managed to get a large paper napkin and procure a pencil from somewhere. We sat in a corner as he drew out a rough plan of the area around the shipping office. When he had finished he sat back and looked at it.

'I think there would be only two ways of quickly getting rid of someone,' he said. 'There are plenty of carts and automobile vans along the quayside. He could have been put in one of those and transported elsewhere.'

'Or he could have been put on board a ship.'

Rory sucked his teeth, producing a most unpleasant sound. 'Actually, I was going to say they could have thrown him in the water.'

'He would not have gone easily.'

'Knock him out beforehand. He might well have had a heart attack when they tried to apprehend him.'

I decided to ignore this last catastrophic suggestion. 'Either they would have needed several men to have lowered him slowly, or they would have had to have been prepared to make a large splash. Either of these would have drawn attention. We had the luxury of withdrawing from the rain, but the dockers and suppliers did not.'

'If he was put in a van he could have been taken anywhere,' said Rory glumly.

'I do not think he was. Whatever was done, it had to have been done quickly. There was no time to arrange a clever plan. However unlucky Bertram was in running into someone who had reason to ... we are missing the point. Why did they take Bertram?'

'I am not missing any point, Euphemia. I am trying to act in a timely manner,' answered Rory shortly.

'It must mean something happened to Fitzroy at these docks. Do you realise he may never have got on the liner at all? He may still be alive! He may be being held prisoner somewhere.' I heard my voice rise with excitement.

'Maybe,' said Rory flatly, 'but I think we should get Bertram back first if we can. You were beginning to say how unlucky Bertram was. Was there a point you were trying to make?'

'Yes,' I said shortly.

'This is no time to be moody,' said Rory. 'Think of your beloved Bertram.'

I bristled, but ignored this. He was right. Time was of the essence. Especially if what I suspected was correct. 'I do not believe for one moment that everyone working at these docks was involved with either the kidnapping of Bertram or Fitzroy. Bertram must have drawn too much attention to himself yesterday when he first went to the office.'

'Quite likely,' said Rory drily.

'He must have made enough noise for whoever did not want enquiries into Fitzroy to continue to have heard about him.'

122

'So you are suggesting that the clerk on duty today was someone involved in whatever the original Fitzroy plot was. That he was waiting to see if Bertram returned.'

I nodded. 'I imagine he was hoping he would not, but he could not take the risk.'

'Would that have been enough time for him to conjure a plan?' asked Rory.

'I imagine that if you have kidnapped someone, not that I ever have, that the last thing you would want to do would be to do the same thing again.'

'Drawing attention to yourself, you mean?' said Rory. 'Bertram is clearly a gentleman of some means and is bound to be missed.'

'Exactly. I imagine that whoever this clerk is, he was hoping he could put Bertram off the scent easily. If he simply confirmed that Fitzroy had boarded the *Titanic* that would have been the end of our enquiries.'

Rory rubbed his hand along his chin. 'When you put it like that, it would have been very easy to get rid of Bertram. I mean simply to tell him that lie and send him on his way. Something must have happened.'

'But you see what I mean about there being no time to make a grand plan? The simplest thing was to give Bertram the lie and send him on his way.'

'But something went wrong,' said Rory.

'Obviously, and the clerk had to handle a situation he did not expect.'

'Well, it would not have been too hard to knock Bertram out,' said Rory. 'Not if you had any experience with that sort of thing. But what would

123

you do with the body?'

I looked out at the busy dock. It was so obvious now I understood. 'They put him on a ship,' I said. 'Tied up, I would imagine, and hidden somewhere where he would not be discovered until he was out at sea.'

Rory's eyes widened. 'Even if they believed he had been put aboard against his will, the captain would not turn the ship around for him.'

'No,' I said, 'and that means it would have bought the clerk and his allies more time.'

Rory gave a low whistle. 'So Fitzroy is still alive.'

'It seems likely.'

'But how do we work out which ship Bertram is on. And more to the point where he has been put?'

'I think I have an idea,' I said, 'but I can guarantee Bertram is not going to like it.'

Rory gave an evil grin.

'This is sounding better and better,' he said.

Chapter Eighteen

In which I make an exhibition of myself at the docks

'So you're telling me your little brother is stowing away on board one of these ships.'

The harbourmaster was a tall craggy man, whose face had been so weathered by the sea his age could have been anything between thirty and fifty-five. He wore a tightly curled beard, but my impression was this was out of necessity from the battering of cruel winds at sea rather than any sartorial sense. His harbourmaster's hat was jammed down tightly over his head, so that he appeared to have no ears. His eyes were wide, blue, and filled with suspicion.

'My brother is a full thirty-three years of age,' I said slowly and clearly. 'But he has the mental age of a small child. He sounds like a man, but this is completely misleading.'

'He is prone to tantrums,' added Rory. 'And when he is in a rage can be a danger to himself or others.'

I flashed him a look of alarm. The last thing we wanted was for the harbourmaster to decide he had to get the police involved.

'Not that he would mean to hurt anyone,' I said quickly.

'Aye, disn't ken his ain strength,' said Rory becoming gruffly Scotch under my rebuke.

'And this is him, is it?' said the harbour master picking up the sketch Rory had done for him. 'Is a good likeness?'

'Yes,' I said truthfully. Rory's talent was as obvious as it was surprising.

'Right, I'd better round up some men,' said the harbourmaster. 'I have more than one ship going out on the tide in an hour.'

'You won't hurt him, will you?' I asked with real fear in my voice.

'Might be better if you came along, sir,' he said to Rory. 'Help calm him down if necessary.'

Rory and I exchanged a look.

125

'To be honest,' he said, 'it's his sister that's best at that. I tend to enrage him more often than not. Seeing as how I am often called to restrain him.'

'Right,' said the harbourmaster, 'if you're used to restraining him you are definitely coming with us. We'll call you, miss, if we need to talk him out from somewhere.'

'Thank you,' I said sincerely. I could only pray that Bertram was unconscious when they found him. If the pretence was that he was a stowaway I hoped that they had not tied him up. That would led to the most awkward of questions and as yet I could think of no response.

At least this time I was waiting in the harbourmaster's office. It was not as warm as the tearoom, but the seats were comfortable and the views out of the window unhampered by steam.

The rain had continued to slow and was now no more than a relentless drizzle. Fog hovered on the horizon, but far enough out, that I had a good view of the open expanse of sea beyond. Before I had sailed with Hans and Richenda such a view would have gladdened and uplifted me. Now I knew that no matter how beautiful the sea might seem she could be wild and cruel. There were two liners in dock. The dockside itself was now awash with both the suppliers loading the ships and the passengers arriving for their voyages. The harbour-master's office allowed both draughts and sound to pass freely through and I heard the excited exclamations of those seeing their ship for the first time. With the fate of the *Titanic* so few months behind us it surprised me that so many people were still so eager for sea travel.

I knew the White Star Line had seemingly been ruthless in distancing itself from the disaster. All the surviving crew and staff had been relieved of their employment the next day, so no one on one of the White Star ships would find themselves sailing with a 'Jonah'.

The thought of Bertram being unwillingly, unwittingly, sent out to sea made the pit of my stomach lurch. To the best of my knowledge he had never sailed before, and his home in the Fens had engendered in him a deep dislike of all forms of unconfined water. I feared his finding himself suddenly at sea might bring on a heart attack – if his capture had not already done so. I knew he would be furious at my ruse to find him, but I would so much rather bear his wrath than see him further endangered.

There was nothing for me to do for the moment but worry. I would have much rather been out looking for him, but I knew all too well how large these ships were. The cargo ships that were also in dock I assumed would be vastly cavernous inside; the cargo bays as large and dark as any unlit cathedral.

The enormity of all the ships unsettled me. That structures much larger than most buildings on land should pitch and roll their way across the depths of the ocean awakened a primeval fear. But perhaps if one had not been associated with a disaster at sea one could forget the darkness beneath. Perhaps Bertram would awaken and think only of the sumptuousness of his surroundings. If we failed to find him perhaps he would find the motion of the sea gentle and reassuring.

The thoughts turned round and over in my head. I felt nauseous and dizzy. The drinks from the tea-shop must have been even poorer than they had tasted. The draughts in here were bad enough that I was shivering. I must have indeed presented a sorry sight when, what felt like hours later, a docker burst through the door.

'Are you the man's sister, ma'am?' he asked. 'You're badly needed.'

I had been sitting still for so long that my legs shook when I stood and I almost fell.

'Is he alive?' I asked.

'Aye, ma'am,' said the docker with a grin. 'He's certainly that.'

These words seemed to bring strength back to my limbs. 'I'm ready,' I said.

'Would you mind if we ran, ma'am?' asked the young docker. 'Only it's urgent.'

'Lead the way,' I said, and hitched up my skirts to a degree that would have made even my lion-hearted mother faint.

We ran across the docks in the direction of one of the cargo ships. 'Make way! Make way! Coming through!' the docker cried. People scattered before us. As a number of dockers who were not involved in the search called out comments, I tried hard not to hear and I am fairly sure one older lady crumpled in shock as I flashed by. My ankles were on display for all to see and I did not care. My mother had been right being involved with the Staplefords had not been good for my moral well-being, but I was so afraid of what I might find on that cargo ship. I needed to know. I needed to get there as fast as I could. It could

128

be that only I could divert Bertram's fury and thus negate the risk of a heart attack. What were bare ankles compared to a man's life?

The boy in front of me pelted up a gangway and I followed. The wooden platform bounced under our feet. The gangway led directly into the side of the ship, so that at the top I hesitated to allow my eyes to adjust to the gloom. The boy ran between a number of loaded pallets and disappeared. I followed and soon found myself at the top of a short ladder. There was nothing for it: I would have to shimmer down and hope that no one at the bottom was watching. I scooped my skirts up over my arm and holding on with one hand managed to climb awkwardly down. I was now in a narrow, metal corridor. I saw the boy waiting a decent distance ahead on the other side of an oval bulkhead door. 'In 'ere, ma'am,' he called.

I rushed over to find a small room so filled with people that I could not enter. It was a cold storage place of some sort. There were sacks and shelves filled with all sorts of things. We must have been below the waterline because the air was decidedly chilly. Backed up against one wall was Bertram, his hair and eyes wild. He was holding a large knife in front of him. Rory was engaged in trying to reason with him, but his voice was getting louder and louder and more and more Scotch. The harbourmaster and three dockers had edged round the side. I glimpsed at least one cudgel.

'What on earth is going on?' I cried.

The harbourmaster's head whipped round. 'What the damnation is she doing down here?'

'You said to fetch help!' said the young docker.

129

'And she was the only one in the office. I thought you meant her.'

The harbourmaster's eyes widened. 'Did you climb down here in those skirts?' he asked, I felt somewhat indelicately.

'I certainly didn't take them off,' I responded tartly. 'Now, what seems to be the problem? I am glad to see you have found my brother and that he appears to be well. Why have you not brought him off the ship?' I said trying my best to imitate the *grande dame* that my mother could do so well. I tuned my tone to that of nurse and demanded, 'And why on earth do you have a knife, Bertram? That is not acceptable behaviour. Put it down.'

'Get out, Euphemia,' yelled Bertram. 'Save yourself. They are murderers and kidnappers.'

'Don't be silly, dear,' I said, trying to convey the message he needed to play with my eyes to Bertram. 'These nice men have helped me find you. And you know Rory. He would never hurt you.'

It seemed to me that the tension in the room was lessening slightly. Certainly, the cudgels had been tucked back out of sight. I hoped my teacherly no-nonsense approach was making them all feel just a little stupid.

However, Bertram did not put his knife down.

'Don't you understand, Euphemia?' he roared. 'These men knocked me out and locked me up down here. Now, they have come to finish me off.'

'Nonsense,' I tried again to indicate that he needed to play along. 'No one has harmed you.'

'I suppose I hit myself on the back of the head,' snapped back Bertram. 'I have a tremendous bump and there is blood in my hair.'

'That explains it,' I said kindly. 'You must have fallen. It is very dark in the cargo hold.'

Bertram began to protest again, but I quickly spoke over him. 'I will take you to see Dr Fitzroy,' I said loudly. 'You know how he always makes you better.'

Bertram looked quite manic at this, but then suddenly his expression changed. 'Dr Fitzroy,' he said. 'You mean this whole situation is down to Dr Fitzroy?'

'Indeed,' I replied, 'and no matter how much these men want to help you none of them work with Dr Fitzroy or his friends.'

'Oh, right,' said Bertram. He handed the knife to Rory. 'Sorry, old chap. Blow to the head confused me a bit like Euphemia said. Can we leave now?'

'Certainly,' I said, 'but if you gentlemen will please do me the courtesy of giving me a head start? Ladders and skirts do not mix well.'

There was a degree of embarrassed shuffling, and the last vestiges of male bravado faded from the room.

Chapter Nineteen

In which a good dinner is ruined by discussion

By the time we reached the hotel it became clear that Bertram had suffered a severe blow to the head. Rory helped him upstairs and I summoned the hotel doctor. He was able to assure us that the chances were that Bertram would not suffer lasting damage, but that he required complete bed rest for at least the rest of the day, if not tomorrow as well. He also suggested that someone should sit with him, so that should he become nauseous or further confused a doctor could be called at once. It was on the tip of my tongue to ask what such changes would mean, but I decided I would rather not know.

'I'll stay with him, Doctor,' said Rory. 'I am sure the hotel will allow a cot bed or some such thing to be brought in under the circumstances.'

'How did he come by the injury?' asked the doctor.

'He fell,' I said quickly.

'Rushing down steps,' added Rory. 'Man is always in a hurry.' He made the mildly disgruntled noise of a servant who finds his master tiresome.

'So he was not inebriated or in a fight?'

'Goodness, no!' I said. 'My brother is not that kind of man.'

The doctor lowered his eyebrows and appeared to consider me for a moment. 'In that case I will advise the hotel of your requirements and ensure they comply. I imagine there will be an extra charge.'

'Oh, that is not an issue,' I said, careless of Bertram's expenses. He had never appeared to be short of money, so I assumed he could easily pay whatever charges were incurred. Rory gave me a curious look.

The doctor left us shortly afterwards. Bertram was muttering under his breath.

'That's nae guid,' said Rory. 'If he comes round I will have a devil of a time convincing him not to come down for dinner.'

'I will leave. He is more likely to argue with me than you.'

Rory sniffed meaningfully. 'If you say so.'

I made my escape. I made my way down the corridor to my room. I knew I would be very hungry later when my excitement and confusion from the day wore away, but at this moment I wanted nothing more than to wash the smells of the dock from hair and skin, and to rest upon a comfortable bed.

When I reached my door I found that my key would not turn in the lock. I stood there, stupefied. Could it be that I had been wrong about Bertram's finances, and that White Orchards had consumed all of his wealth? Were we about to be thrown out upon the street?

Panic flared within my chest, but then just as quickly faded. The key in my hand bore a very different number to the one upon the door. I had come to the wrong room. I had gone in the direction of my room at the previous hotel. Clearly, I was more shaken by the day's events than I realised. I turned, and with some effort managed to retrace my steps to my room. As I did so I realised that something was different. When I opened my door, the key having worked this time, I saw quite clearly that the carpet in the hallway was a great deal brighter in colour than the one in my room. I had paid it no attention this morning, but clearly last night a new carpet had been laid. The new pattern was exactly the same as the one in the previous hotel.

I spent no more time thinking about the hotel, but summoned water for washing. Having completed by ablutions, I undid my stays and laid down upon the bed. I had the forethought to ask the maid to knock me up in good time for dinner.

Much later, rested and revived, I made my way down to the dining room. I trusted Rory would summon me should anything be amiss with Bertram. My disturbing them would only add to the time Bertram needed to recover. I thought it likely he remained some way from forgiving me my ruse and that my presence would only agitate him.

The thought of a solitary supper did not depress me. After all the excitements of the last few days some quiet solitude would be most welcome. But it was not to be. Barely had I placed my hand upon the dining room doorknob when a waiter appeared at my side and redirected me to a smaller room.

'Your companions are awaiting you here, Miss,'

he said opening the door. Seated at the table I saw Rory, thankfully not in his servant's livery, and a whey-faced Bertram. 'I will give you a moment to consult the menu,' said the waiter and shut the door behind me.

'Dinnae be blaming me,' said Rory. 'If they had not put down that new carpet he would never have thought of it.'

'Have you also suffered a blow to the head?' I asked Rory coldly.

'I would be careful how you answer that,' said Bertram, 'or she will be about giving you a head injury yourself.'

'As if I would be so uncouth,' I said, sitting down opposite them and frowning in annoyance.

'Oh, I don't know,' said Bertram, 'I heard Euphemia flashed her ankles for the whole docks to see. That seems mightily uncouth to me.'

I raised my eyebrows in surprise. I was not used to Bertram making this kind of comment.

'Are you sure you are well enough to be at dinner?' I asked. 'The doctor did suggest...'

'Pah!' interrupted Bertram. 'I've been made a fool of twice today. I will not lie back and ... and ... take it.'

'I can quite see how eating soup will prove you more manly,' I said.

Bertram scowled ferociously and scratched at his beard with vigour.

'Don't do that! Not at the dinner table!' I exclaimed in horror. 'It is far from hygienic.'

'Euphemia,' rumbled Bertram as ire built up inside him like steam in a kettle, 'What the devil were you thinking...'

135

'I was thinking only of how we could find you quickly before the ship set sail. A circumstance I suspect your assailants were counting upon.'

'What gets me,' said Rory, 'is why they did not just drop you off the end of the quay. It would have been far less risky and most likely it would have been thought an accident.'

I nodded. 'It is odd.'

'I am sorry to disappoint you both,' said Bertram, but neither Rory or I paid any attention to him.

'It is the same with the clerk not simply saying that Fitzroy had got on the boat. That would have completely ended our investigation.'

'I suspect the clerk may have panicked,' I said. 'Presumably he has been paid off to turn a blind eye to certain things. But that is a long way short from arranging fatal accidents or even lying to investigation officers. Do you think they thought you were from the police, Bertram?'

'Good God, Euphemia. I am a gentleman!'

'What you say would lead to the conclusion that there is more than one level of criminal involved. There are men who have been bribed at the docks and there are those who actually took Fitzroy away. I can only imagine that removing him from a place against his will would not have been an easy task, and may have involved considerable violence.' Rory's voice had crept back to his correct butler English and away from the Scotch. Obviously sitting in a private dining room was having an effect on him. I rather enjoyed his Scottish burr.

'Euphemia, are you listening to me?'

136

'What? Yes. More than one group of criminals involved. Though I also think it is worth considering that murdering someone inevitably leads to the death penalty. One must be quite desperate to risk that, don't you think?'

'Or a fanatic,' said Bertram darkly. 'Who knows what kind of people would be after Fitzroy.'

'Both Rory and I have seen him kill and display no remorse. He is a most ruthless man.'

'I thought you rather liked him,' said Bertram, scratching his beard again.

'No,' I said shortly. Though the truth was far more complicated.

At this point the waiter reappeared and took our orders for dinner. To my horror Bertram ordered soup. After he had left I could not contain myself. 'Bertram, men who have beards should not order soup. It sticks most unattractively in their whiskers.'

Bertram looked pained. 'I do know how to use a napkin, Euphemia.'

'Yes, but it is fish soup. You will stink all evening.'

Bertram pulled his shoulders back and adopted his most formal expression. 'Then I suggest you do not sniff me.'

'Oh, for heaven's sake,' burst out Rory. 'Forget the soup. What are we going to do? For the life of me I cannae see we have any avenues to follow.'

'Of course, we do,' said Bertram. 'We need to kidnap that clerk–'

The door opened.

'Soup,' announced the waiter.

137

Chapter Twenty

In which a carpet is much to blame

The courses came quick and fast, so that neither Rory nor I had the chance to question Bertram's ridiculous declaration until the cheeseboard was borne in.

'If the lady would like to retire to the ladies' lounge,' said the waiter, 'I will serve tea and bring port for the gentlemen.'

'*This* lady will drink port,' announced Bertram.

A barely detectable shiver ran through the waiter. 'As you wish, sir,' he said in lowered tone.

'A woman who drinks port and a man who dines with his chauffeur. Ach, the stories you two have started,' said Rory, helping himself to the port that the waiter had silently and disapprovingly deposited on the table.

'A lady, if you do not mind,' I said.

'Ach, Euphemia, dinnae go getting ideas above yer station,' said Rory.

I started. 'Of course,' I said as contritely as I could. Rory had no idea of my real connections, but the more I socialised above stairs the more I lapsed back into the manner my mother had cultivated in me. I needed to be more careful.

'I think you are a lady,' said Bertram.

'Yes,' I replied, 'but you want to embark on a criminal career, so I am not entirely sure your

138

opinion can be counted.'

'Yes,' said Rory, 'what are ye on about?'

'Remember how I said the new carpet gave me an idea?' Bertram said.

'Yes,' said Rory, 'it made you want to come down to dinner. And while the pattern is not to my taste either...'

'No, no, no,' said Bertram. 'It gave me an idea about how to steal a body. We could wrap it in the carpet.'

Rory and I regarded him wordlessly.

'We give the clerk the same treatment he gave me. We knock him on the head, but we remove him from the dock and make him tell us who bribed him. It is the only way we can move forward with this. If we honestly think Fitzroy may still be alive and in danger, then we must make haste to locate him.'

'Do you know anything about knocking people out?' I asked.

Bertram rubbed his head. 'I have first-hand experience. You just need something hard and thwack to the back of the head and they're out.'

'Do you not think you might as easily kill them?' I said.

'That's nae the problem,' said Rory. He shifted uncomfortably in his seat, 'I was a wee bittie wild as a lad. Brawls are common enough among young Highland folk.' He took a deep breath. 'Nae, the real problem is how we get to the clerk in the first place.'

'The docks are open all night,' said Bertram. 'We will have to watch and see when he comes on night duty. A man desperate enough to take a bribe is not likely to stay away from his work. He obviously needs the money.'

'I'll grant you the docks are quieter at night,' said Rory, 'but you really think could get him away in a carpet?'

'An old carpet,' said Bertram. 'One that could have been recently replaced on a ship. We would have to wear overalls, or some sort of dockers' clothing.'

Rory pondered this. 'Early morning would probably be best if we were pretending to be from one of the suppliers. They start early, but the docks would be fairly quiet then. It would be risky, aye, but if we acted with enough confidence, it might just work.'

'Good man!' exclaimed Bertram.

'I absolutely forbid it,' I cried.

'That's a bit rich, coming from you, Euphemia,' said Bertram. 'You're the reason we are here in the first place.'

'I really do appreciate all the support you have both given me,' I said, 'but I cannot let you endanger yourselves in this way.'

'So you are not fundamentally opposed to us breaking the law?' said Rory.

I blushed.

'Of course I am,' I said, though it had been the furthest thing from my mind.

Rory eyed me closely. 'Aye, right.'

He turned to Bertram. 'She's just upset because she thinks we willnae let her come on the kidnapping.'

'Of course, we won't,' said Bertram outraged. 'That would be no place for a lady.'

140

I put my head in my hands. I trembled to think of what this pair would get up to unsupervised. I raised my head. 'Bertram,' I said pleadingly, 'you would not even be considering this if you had not been knocked out. You are not yourself. Your brains are bruised.'

'There is nothing wrong with my brain,' snapped Bertram, 'I feel in excellent health. You may have noted that despite the rigours of the day I have not had any difficulty with my heart. I do believe that the Fens have done me the world of good, and I am stronger and fitter than I have ever been before.'

'Do you agree?' I asked Rory. He would not meet my eyes.

'Aye, well, if my master's going.'

'Oh, you are as bad as one another,' I said. 'I am going up to bed. I am sure a good night's sleep will help us all, and what we can do will be clearer in the morning.' I rose.

Rory opened his mouth to speak.

'Good idea,' interrupted Bertram. 'I shall treat Rory to a cigar for all his help.' Rory frowned and I left them before another argument could break out.

Chapter Twenty-one

In which Rory and Bertram indulge themselves in a little *quid pro quo*

I awoke refreshed. The light shining through my window was bright and promised a lovely warm summer's day. I opened the window a little and the delightful smell of sea air wafted in. I dressed quickly. I still had little idea of how we could move forward. Though I was entertaining some idea of trying to bribe the truth from the clerk. Surely if he had been willing to turn his back on his dockland employers, he might also be persuaded to do so against his criminal masters for a further monetary remuneration?

Of one thing I was certain: if the three of us put our heads together we could come up with a solution. We had achieved so much when we worked together that I was not prepared to admit defeat now. I would need to show both men how much I appreciated them. A little flattery would surely bring them round to my side.

I tripped down to breakfast feeling more optimistic than I had for days. Fitzroy might yet be alive, and the three of us were back working together.

I saw Bertram seated at a table in the dining room. He was pouring himself coffee. There were a number of discarded plates before him. He had

142

obviously eaten well. As I approached the table he rose and held out my chair for me.

'Good morning, Euphemia,' he said with a most happy smile.

'You look as if you are feeling much recovered,' I said, pleased.

'Never felt better in my life,' said Bertram and indeed he did appear to be brimming with vigour.

'Has something excited you?' I asked confused.

'Have your breakfast, Euphemia,' said Bertram. 'I recommend the eggs Benedict. Excellent this morning.'

I ordered as he suggested and Bertram asked for another pot of coffee.

'It is a glorious day,' I said in the friendliest manner I could.

'Indeed,' said Bertram, 'Rory is going to take us for a drive after breakfast.'

'I wondered where he was,' I said.

'When you are ready we shall go round to meet the automobile.'

I thought this a little curious. Usually one summoned the vehicle to the front steps, but perhaps Bertram was trying to make Rory feel less like a servant while we worked together. It was only later, after an excellent breakfast, and a lovely short walk in the sun, that I saw the roll of carpet protruding from the baggage compartment.

'Oh, good God in heaven,' I exclaimed, 'you didn't!' I had, of course, been a complete idiot. While I was tucked up in bed, my two companions had been off attempting to prove their manliness down at the docks.

Bertram gave me a wide grin, 'Oh, yes, we did.

143

Now, climb in. We need to find somewhere to inspect our new carpet.' For the first time in my life I was truly speechless.

Rory drove us inland towards the countryside. It was not long before we left the town behind. Afterwards we passed through several small hamlets and gradually the land around us became more and more deserted. Bertram rapped on the glass and directed Rory to leave the official road and drive down some narrow tree-lined country lanes. Eventually, he turned into a field and parked beside a small copse of trees. The view stretched out for ever, flat and wide. We could clearly see that no one else was around for miles.

'You know this place?' I asked Bertram. It was so perfect for his intent.

'Found it when we were driving around this morning. As you could not come on the first part of the exercise I thought it was only fair you be included in the second half. Besides, you may well have a better idea of what to ask than us. You are the one who has been reading Fitzroy's correspondence and the one who knew him best.' The last phrase was said with a slight frown. However, I did not think Bertram was jealous, so much as disapproving. Something, which considering his most recent actions, struck me as distinctly laughable. 'I will just go and help Rory get him out.'

'Has he been in that roll all night?' I said horrified. 'Are you sure he is still alive?'

'Oh, he will be fine,' said Bertram blithely. 'Our man here did not hit him that hard, and he has only been wrapped up a couple of hours.'

He went over to the rear of the vehicle and he

and Rory heaved and hefted the carpet onto the grass. It landed with a loud thud. Before I could protest, the two of them pulled at the edge and the carpet unrolled depositing a bound, gagged man, onto the grass. He was not wearing a blindfold. When I saw this I could happily have knocked Rory and Bertram on their heads myself.

'He can see us,' I hissed.

Bertram looked at me blankly. 'It was dark in the carpet. I did not see any need to blindfold him.'

'It is not dark now,' I said coldly.

'No,' said Bertram. 'It is a lovely day.'

'She means,' said Rory, 'that the man has seen our faces. Sorry. I should have thought of that.'

'Oh well,' said Bertram blithely. 'We will have to kill him.'

I blanched.

'Unless he tells us what we want to know,' he said. He pulled a pocket knife from his trousers and knelt down beside the man.

The clerk was not a tall man. A rug might have sufficed as easily as the carpet. He had a slight build, short brown hair not recently washed, acne vulgaris on his cheeks, and a weaselly look about him. I judged him to be in his early twenties and of a most unsound character. He had weak, watery blue eyes that were currently staring fixedly at the knife in Bertram's hand. Bertram brought the knife closer to his face and the little man squeaked.

Rory had come up beside me. In a low voice, 'I think that blow to the head has affected Bertram more than I thought. He was very courageous last night.'

145

'You mean foolhardy,' I said in an urgent whisper. 'What on earth are we to do with this man once we have the information we need? Presuming he has it to give in the first place.'

Bertram slid his knife under the gag and in one swift movement cut through it. It fell away from the clerk's face and he gulped down air. Sweat broke out on his forehead.

'I am sure you would like a drink,' said Bertram pleasantly. 'If my friend and I prop you up against this tree trunk I will fetch some water from the vehicle.'

Rory obeyed this summons. Bertram held a small flask to the man's lips and let him drink a little. 'There you go,' he said. 'I do not want you to think we are monsters. Now, my friends here would like to ask you some questions.'

The clerk finally found his voice. It was slightly higher than most males', and had an intrinsic nasal whine that was most annoying.

'You had better let me go,' he said. 'I have friends, powerful friends. The things they would do to you. The things they could do to that girl.'

He leered at me. Rory stepped forward and struck him across the face. I gasped.

'You will keep a civil tongue in your head,' Rory said. 'You are in the presence of a lady.'

A trickle of blood formed at the corner of the man's mouth and ran down his chin. Bertram turned a shocked face towards me. All his bravado had vanished. I saw now he had been play-acting. Now the situation had become all too real.

'Who bribed you to tell them if anyone came asking for...' I hesitated. I did not know what name he knew Fitzroy by. 'This man,' finished Bertram, pulling Rory's drawing from his pocket.'

'I'm not telling you nothing,' said the clerk. 'As soon as yous have got what you want you'll ditch me.'

'I would have thought you would like us to "ditch" you,' I said.

The clerk sneered. 'New to this, are you? Or haven't your boyfriends told you they cannot let me live.'

Wordlessly, Rory struck the man in the face again. Bertram went a little paler.

'I'll give you my word that you will not be killed if you give us the information we seek,' I said.

'They obey your orders, do they? Have a way of keeping them under control, do you?' The last words were said with the most obvious sleazy intent. This time neither Bertram or I flinched when Rory struck him again.

'We are a team,' I said quietly. 'We are seeking this individual and you may be surprised at how much we are prepared to do to locate him.'

'What's he done to you?' asked the clerk.

'He is an agent of His Majesty's Government,' I said coldly.

'Oh, cripes!' said the clerk, the first look of real alarm crossing his face. 'Government stuff. You're not from the tax office, are you?'

'Much, much worse,' I said softly.

'Yes, one's worst nightmares and all that,' said Bertram.

'My colleagues are attempting to inform you that we will get the information we need from you one way or another. How difficult this situation becomes is entirely down to you. I am prepared to ask the lady to wait in the automobile if necessary,' said Rory in a voice as cold as iron.

Bertram gave me a look that said he would rather like to get in the automobile with me.

'National interests,' said Rory.

'Right,' said the clerk. 'I wouldn't want you to think I was unpatriotic.'

'Of course not,' said Rory. 'We hang people for treason in his country.'

'Look,' said the clerk, beginning to gabble. 'They told me it was all about the contracts for supplying the ships. I thought it was criminal, not treasonous.'

'They are plotting against the King,' said Rory.

'Cor blimey,' said the clerk. 'At a pig farm?'

'Treason can be committed anywhere,' said Rory.

'Pig farm?' I interjected.

'Yes, they supply the sausages, bacon, and carcasses to the liners. Top quality pork.'

'Pinch me,' whispered Bertram in my ear.

'You are not dreaming,' I hissed back. Then to the man I said, 'Which farm?'

'Perfect Piggy Provisions,' said the clerk, his eyes wide.

'If you're making this up...' warned Rory.

'I'm not! I'm not!' squeaked the clerk in alarm. 'You must have seen one of their vans around here. They have a pig in a top hat on the side.'

'No one could make that up,' said Bertram.

'What are you going to do with me now?' asked the clerk.

'You are going to take us to buy some pork,'

148

said Rory. 'Bertram, help me get him back in the vehicle.'

'He is not going in the back with us,' protested Bertram.

'The lady can sit up front with me. You need to be in the back to keep an eye on him.'

'Me?' protested the clerk. 'I'm trussed up like a goose on Christmas Eve.'

'Well, behave yourself then,' said Rory. 'Or we'll put you in the oven.'

Chapter Twenty-two

In which we take a trip into the countryside and Bertram makes good use of his shoe

I climbed into the front of the automobile next to Rory. Bertram relayed directions he gained from the clerk through the speaking tube, but neither of them could hear Rory and my conversation.

'What on earth do you think you are doing?' I protested.

'I am doing what you wanted,' said Rory. 'I am doing my best to free this Fitzroy chap.'

'But we cannot take on – *take on!* – whoever they are. We are not Fitzroys.'

'I dinnae see we have much option,' said Rory, lapsing back into Scots. 'Frae what ye telt me his whole department think the mannie deid. And we certainly cannae go tae the pol-ice. It down to

149

us. Unless ye want to let the man die.'

'Damn Fitzroy,' I said with feeling.

'Say the word and I will happily turn the automobile around and leave him to his fate.'

'And the clerk?'

'Och, if we leave him in the countryside somewhere there's no reason he should ever be able to find us. Even Bertram has had the sense not to use our names.'

I sighed. 'We cannot just leave him to die.'

'The countryside isnae that fierce around here.'

'I meant Fitzroy,' I said.

'He's in a shady line of work. He kens the risks.'

'Then why did he leave an instruction to me to check if he was really dead.'

'Maybe he thought you would be the only one who would care,' said Rory. 'I dinnae ken how close the twa of yous have become.'

'Not at all,' I said coldly.

'And yet he asks you.'

'Oh, for Heaven's sake, Rory, now is not the time for one of your jealous fits of temper. You jilted me, remember.'

'Ainely because you were too guid for me. And I'm ten times the man Fitzroy will ever be. Slimy devil that he is.'

At this point we were interrupted by Bertram informing us the farm was around the next bend. Rory took the automobile off the road and found a place behind a hedge were we could see the farm from a distance. It was far, far bigger than I had imagined. I was distracted from the sight by the sound of movement behind me. I turned round and to my astonishment saw Bertram pulling a large picnic basket out of the baggage compartment. He lugged it round to the front the vehicle. 'Hie, Euphemia, come and help me set this up,' he called.

'So much for not using names,' said Rory. Bertram had left his door open. I scrambled down and went over to help him.

'Anyone who sees us will only think we are having a picnic,' said Bertram. 'You see, Rory and I did think of everything.'

I laid out a tablecloth, set out china plates of dainty sandwiches, cakes, and tiny pies and pastries. There was a large sealed jug of lemonade, and one of those flasks designed to keep things warm, filled with coffee. There were silver knives and forks, and matching cups and saucers. The hotel seemed to have provided everything for a motorist's lunch. Rory came over to join us on the grass.

'What about the clerk?' I asked.

'He's not going anywhere unless he is very good at hopping,' said Rory. 'I made him a new gag, so he won't be attracting any attention.'

'As it's here,' said Bertram eyeing an iced bun, 'we may as well eat it.'

It transpired that all of us were remarkably hungry after the exertions of the morning. Both men had been up before dawn, so it was not surprising they needed sustenance. I, on the hand, had the lingering feeling that this might be my last meal. When we had eaten and drunk our fill I again raised the question of what we might do next.

'The place is much larger than I imagined,' said Rory, echoing my thoughts. 'I had hoped it would have only a few outbuildings and we might be able to work out where they were holding Fitzroy.'

'And?' I asked.

'We had got as far as thinking about coming back after dark to rescue him,' said Bertram.

'How?' I asked.

'Oh, knocking out guards and knocking down doors. That sort of thing,' said Bertram airily.

'If they have weapons?'

'We were going to wait until the guards were not around,' said Bertram. 'If there even were guards.' He frowned at me. 'You are being rather difficult, Euphemia.'

'I am sitting having a picnic in front of car that contains a kidnapped man, and in a field next to a pig farm peopled with traitors. I think the whole situation is rather difficult,' I said dryly.

'It might be a good idea if we got a closer look at the farm, so we could see what we are up against,' said Rory.

'How?' I asked. Bertram scowled at me and scratched his beard in a most irritating manner. I sighed and said, 'I suggest that one or two of us fabricate a pretext for calling at the farm and make the most of the opportunity to discover the lay of the land.'

'That's you and me, then,' said Bertram to Rory.

'Actually, I think it would seem more harmless if I took Euphemia with me,' said Rory. 'I need you to guard the clerk. If someone comes by you might have to untie him, so everything looks normal, and still keep him under control.'

'How the devil would I do that?' demanded Bertram.

'I have no idea,' said Rory. 'I only know we cannot ask Euphemia to do it.'

'Damn Fitzroy,' said Bertram. 'Are you sure, Euphemia, that we can't just throw in the towel and go home? I am beginning to get the devil of a headache.'

'We should give our prisoner something to eat,' I said.

Rory shrugged. 'Give him the fish paste sandwiches. They are below the standard I would have expected from the hotel. I shall have to have words.'

'Perhaps we are the housekeeper and butler of a Lord, who is opening a house down here and wants us to assess the local produce.'

'Then you had better be the cook.'

'But I know nothing about cooking!' I protested.

'Fortunately for us, as my uncle was the local butcher and I know more about meat than most men.'

'Did your family run the entire High Street?' asked Bertram. 'You certainly appear to have mercantile ancestors.'

'Aye,' said Rory darkly.

'Best plan is you say as little as possible, Euphemia. We had better be husband and wife for this too.'

I nodded. 'That is much more believable.'

'I don't like this,' said Bertram. 'You will be walking into a den of traitors.'

'This was never going to be easy,' I said. 'We have come too far to turn back now.'

'No, we haven't,' protested Bertram. 'My automobile will turn around as easy as a hot knife goes through jam.'

'Butter,' Rory and I corrected at once.

'It was Fitzroy who brought Euphemia into this,' said Rory. 'I second your desire to shield her from danger, but I think we are all in great danger until we retrieve Fitzroy. Once we have him, I am hoping he can handle the situation.'

'As well as he is handling it now,' muttered Bertram.

'At least he should be able to summon reinforcements,' said Rory.

One thought had been troubling me for some time. 'We kept pigs when I was child,' I said. 'Pigs eat anything.'

'Yes,' said Bertram. 'Do you want to take them some of this? Only I don't think bribing a pig with a jam tart is liable to help us much.'

'No, she means that a good way to get rid of a body is to chop it up and feed it to pigs,' said Rory.

'But people eat those pigs!' cried Bertram. He dropped his head in his hands. 'That is so wrong.'

'Murder generally is,' I said.

'I will never look at another sausage the same way,' said Bertram with great regret.

'Devastated as I am for your loss,' said Rory, 'if Euphemia and I are going to go in we had better do it now before the afternoon is spent. Obviously, we will need to take the automobile.'

Bertram sat up as if he had been stung by a bee. 'Of course,' I said. 'It is not as if we can appear out of nowhere. It has to be believable that we have come from a nearby big house. Do you know the names of any?'

Rory shook his head. 'I did look up a few of them on the map, and enquire among the hotel staff. I said I needed to change masters.'

Bertram grumbled under his breath, but Rory spoke over him.

'However, upon consideration it occurs to me that the farmers may already have made arrangements with the local houses, and we would immediately be exposed.'

'What am I meant to do with our prisoner?' demanded Bertram. 'Or are you intending to take him with you?'

Rory gave him a look which quite clearly told him not to be so stupid, but all he said was, 'I think the best situation is if we lie him down and put the rug over him. You can lean on him as if he is part of your picnic equipment. If anyone questions you, you can say your companions have gone to fetch more beer from the local public house.'

'Do I look like the kind of man who drinks beer in fields?!'

But Rory was already heading to the automobile to retrieve the prisoner.

'Would you like me to clear any of this away?' I asked Bertram indicating the picnic.

'Leave it. It seems the only employment I am to be allowed to have is to eat jam and scones in the sun.'

'That will be a lot nicer than walking around a smelly pig farm,' I responded.

'That smell,' asked Bertram, 'is that them?'

'Yes, what did you think it was?'

Bertram blushed slightly. 'I really didn't want

to say. The Scotch do eat some funny things.'

Rory appeared towing a hopping clerk. 'Lie down there,' he commanded. The clerk looked at us helpless for a moment. Then toppled over head long like a falling tree. His head struck the ground hard and his eyes closed. Rory threw the carpet over him. 'That should keep him out of your way.'

I followed Rory back to the automobile aware that I was leaving a very disgruntled Bertram behind me.

'Are you sure you want me to accompany you,' I said as I climbed into the seat beside the driver. 'Would it not make more sense to have a strong man with you?'

Rory started the engine and climbed up beside me. 'Do you know where I could find one?' he asked.

'Oh, that is cruel.'

'Bertram Stapleford is an intelligent and a brave man,' he said. 'But he is far from being in good health. Leaving his heart condition aside, he is still suffering from concussion. The normal Bertram would not have gone along with any of these schemes.'

'I did wonder.'

'Plus you are better at thinking on your feet. Bertram has a tendency to panic.'

'He has led a sheltered life,' I said defensively.

'Oh, he's better than most toffs,' said Rory. 'I will give you that.'

And with that he drove the vehicle out of the field. My last sight of Bertram was a view of him attempting to beat back a rising carpet with his shoe.

Chapter Twenty-three

In which I wait a very long time for a cup of tea

The stench of the pig farm lodged deep in our nostrils before we even turned into the farm driveway. I took a handkerchief from my bag and held it to my nose.

'Och, be careful, Euphemia,' said Rory. 'You're not pretending to be a lady the now.'

'I do wish you would decide to speak in either the King's English or Scotch,' I quibbled. 'This constant changing is most confusing.'

'Aye, I can see that,' said Rory. 'I reckon I am stuck between the twa now. It used to be English for work and Scots – Scots that is, Euphemia, not Scotch. Scotch is something you drink. Anyway, Scots was for home. But I'm becoming more like yourself. A fish out of water.'

This came dangerously near to the truth, so I let the topic slide. 'So what is the plan?'

'What we discussed. We have come to enquire after meat for a grand meal our master is intending to host to launch himself and his family in the neighbourhood. He is most particular about his meat and has sent us to inspect it.'

'And how do we rescue Fitzroy?'

'We dinnae. At least not yet. The point of this exercise is to get a look around the farm and

157

ascertain where he may be being held. Bertram and I will return later at night and attempt to free him. So as much information we can find out about the lie of the land this time would be most useful.'

I could see a great many problems with this plan. I mentioned one. 'They will doubtless have dogs.'

'Aye, it's a shame. We will have to use poisoned meat.'

'Oh, the poor things.'

'Poor me if I get canine jaws sunk into my ar ... posterior and then shot by the awakened farmers.'

'Yes, I see.' I paused. 'Do you think he is still alive?'

'You mean has he become pig-food yet?'

I nodded.

'I am afraid that our escapades at the docks previously did arouse suspicion and it may be that his captors will cut their losses and run. That is if he has not already told them what they need to know.'

'I think that is unlikely,' I said. 'I cannot imagine him caving under torture.'

Rory threw me a sidelong look.

'You have no idea what torture is,' he said.

'Neither do you,' I replied crisply. 'But we can be certain it would be most unpleasant.'

For a moment it seemed as if Rory had something more to add, but he let the moment pass. He drew up alongside the house. He turned off the engine and jumped down leaving me to fend for myself. The farm drive was exceedingly muddy, so I felt faintly victorious when I managed to

158

scrabble down without ending up head first in the mud.

The farmhouse was a long low building of only one storey. The entire structure was clad with wooden planks, making it look more like a barn than a house. It was a big flat cube of a thing that promised corridors winding between the rooms. There were several windows at the front and two at the side nearest us. They seemed to have been put in a most haphazard manner. The ones that faced out over the farmyard were covered in a wire frame through which would be vaguely glimpsed none-too-clean curtains. Only the side windows near the door were clean and sparkling in the sun. There was a main entrance at the front of the building, but it was clearly shut up.

Before it and around to the side there were rows and rows of pig pens with their small yards. From the one nearest to us it seemed there were either two or three pigs in one or a sow and her piglets. It was a very large operation. I estimated there must have been over a hundred animals on the premises. The noise they made was a loud snuffling and slurping, but it was the smell that was overpowering. The stench of dung ripening in the sun was extremely unpleasant. Away in the distance I could see other covered outbuildings and shut doors. The yard itself was muddy and rutted. It was clear of debris, but somehow still unkempt. Bags of pig feed were piled up alongside the house. A wheelbarrow stood next to them. I gathered we had arrived close to feeding time.

Rory walked up to the side door and banged on it. I followed quickly behind him. The door opened with a hideous squeak, revealing a well-rounded middle-aged woman in a long, faded dress, knocking flour from her hands.

'Can I help you?' she said, sounding and looking all the world like a typical farmer's wife.

'Aye,' said Rory. 'I mean yes.' He too seemed flustered by the woman's homely guise. 'Our master is moving into the neighbourhood and is holding a grand weekend party. He has asked Cook and I to enquire locally about the availability of fine ingredients.'

'I wish I could help, but you have come on my baking day. Derek, my husband, is out feeding the beasts. He'd be happy to call at your house if you will leave your address. He can bring some samples out for you to try.'

'That is a kind offer,' answered Rory, 'but our master is most insistent that we see how the animals are reared. He has some guy modern ideas about farming.'

'How strange,' said the woman noncommittally.

'Aye, he is a strange man, but a wealthy one,' continued Rory. 'In with all the top people, though his is a new title. I believe even the local magistrates will be attending.'

'Will they indeed,' said the woman. 'You had better come in. I will make you a cup of tea while you wait for Derek. I don't have anything to do with the beasts myself. Dirty things. This way. I warn you he may be a while.'

'Perhaps we could look for him among the sties?' asked Rory.

'Oh, you wouldn't want to do that,' said the farmer's wife. 'Some of those beasts can be right

160

vicious. People take the Perfect Piggy name to heart, but really they are nasty things, pigs. You wouldn't want to end up in a pen by mistake. Take a chunk out of your leg soon as look at you, they would. And then once you're on the ground ... well, let's just say it's unlikely you would be getting up again. There, there, dear. You are looking quite pale,' she said, patting me on the arm. 'You sit yourself down in my little parlour. There'll be no piggies coming in here. Our Rufus will see to that won't you, boy?' she finished obscurely.

She had led us into a small, well-kept parlour. A fire was burning in the grate despite the warmness of the day. A clean threadbare couch with hand-quilted cushions set before the hearth. As we approached the hearth rug rose up to meet us, revealing itself to be Rufus, a brown and grey mongrel dog, the size of a small pony. He bared his teeth at the sight of us.

'Don't mind him,' said the woman. 'He's just giving you a smile.'

The dog gave a low, rumbling growl. As one, Rory and I sat down on the couch. 'I'll be back in a minute,' said the woman. 'Make yourself at home.'

Rufus plonked his great haunches down on the ground and sat down opposite us. Seated his and my eye level matched. He was truly huge. A dollop of salvia drooled down towards the floor. I could not help wondering if he had been fed today.

'That's a guy big guard dog,' said Rory quietly. 'Do you think he's half pony?'

'I think he has been set to watch us and make

161

sure we do not leave this room.'

Rory lowered his voice even further. 'Do you think they know who we are?'

'I do not think so,' I said. 'I think she is being as cautious as anyone might be who had a prisoner on the premises. You said we were sent by our master, so they cannot risk making us disappear as our master would come looking for us.'

'That was the idea,' said Rory.

'I was almost convinced we had it all wrong,' I said.

'She is a very convincing farmer's wife.'

'She has not been baking.'

'What?'

'Do you smell bread? She said it was baking day. There's no smell.'

Rory nodded. 'The work of a moment to dip your hands in some flour. These are very dangerous people.'

'I agree,' I said. 'Maybe we should leave before she comes back.' I started to rise. Rufus let out a blood-curdling growl. I sat back down. 'Maybe not,' said Rory. I looked at him helplessly. Everything had already started to go wrong.

What felt like hours later the woman returned, bringing a coarse-looking, squat man with her. There was no sign of any tea things.

'My husband,' she said. 'These people, Derek, are enquiring about your meats for their master.'

Derek grunted and came across to Rufus. He rubbed the dog's ears. Rufus looked up at him adoringly and drooled on his shoe.

'Good boy,' he said to the dog. Then he looked over to us. 'Don't do farm visits,' he said shortly.

'Give me your address and I'll bring some meat round to sample.'

'They said their master wants to see how the beasts are reared,' put in the woman.

'Why?' said the man.

Rory shrugged. 'The man has some ideas about how beasts should be raised. As I said to your wife, he is a guy strange man.'

'Scots, are you?' said Derek. He smiled at Rory. 'Good people, the Scots.'

'We are that,' agreed Rory.

'And what do you think about your master's ideas?'

'I think you should trust the farmer. My father has a smallholding up in the Highlands.'

'So you know a bit about farming.'

'A wee bit,' said Rory.

'I tell you what, seeing as you have farmer's blood in your veins I'll make an exception for you and give you a little tour. Your cook can stay with my wife and have a cup of tea. Tilda never takes enough breaks. Girl would work herself to death if I let her. It will be nice for her to have some company for a while.'

'Excellent,' said Rory. 'It would be grand to see your farm. It looked mighty impressive driving up.' He stood up. This time Rufus made no protest.

'Take Rufus with you,' said his wife. 'I think the girl is a bit shy of him.'

'What, a hulking great softie like him?' said the man, bending down to rub the dog's stomach. 'He wouldn't hurt a fly. Unless they were intruders, like. Best guard dog in the county.'

163

'I can believe it,' I said. 'He is a formidable animal.'

The farmer gave me a smile, but his eyes remained cold. 'You make yourself comfy, girl, and I'll show your man what he wants to see. The wife will bring your tea.'

Rory left with the farmer and Rufus. The woman smiled at me and closed the door behind her. 'I'll fetch the tea,' she called. Then I heard the click of a key being turned. I had been locked in.

Chapter Twenty-four

In which I have a cosy chat with a farmer's wife

I flew out of my seat and tried the door. As I feared, it did not budge. My heart was beating too fast, but I tried to slow my breathing and calm myself. I turned round slowly and assessed my surroundings more clearly. There was no other door. The window had a wire net fastened across it. I also noted that the room had cobwebs around the chimney stack and dirt in the corners. I had never been to a pig farm before, but all the other farmer's wives I had met in my childhood when my father was vicar of Sweet Meadow Parish had taken enormous pride in their homes. Almost as if they were trying to counter the inevitable chaos of the farmyard outside.

This farm did not make sense. There were undeniably many pigs here, but a farmer's wife who pretended to bake? A dirty farmhouse? A man who did not like his animals to be seen? And even the strange layout of the house. The cumulative effect of these facts made me sure that Fitzroy had been, and hopefully was still, kept here.

What shocked me the most was that a woman was involved in his kidnap. But then I was supposedly the head of his rescue operation.

Now, that was laughable. If Fitzroy was to be believed, which was always questionable, he was one of the chief players in his department and involved in affairs of the nation abroad. That he should have Bertram, Rory, and myself as his rescuers boded ill for all of us. If only he had passed on to us a fraction of his skills as opposed to simply hushing us with the Official Secrets Act. A hairpin that had been dislodged by my leaping up fell to the ground. I picked it up. How hard could it be to pick a lock with one of these?

As it turned out, very hard. I ended up snapping the pin in half and spending what felt like a very long time trying to fish the remnants out with the other half before the farmer's wife returned and found the lock jammed.

I ended up with one end in my teeth, while I broke several of my fingernails in the lock and dirtied my skirt on the floor. The actual skill of picking locks had to be easier than this. The final piece fell out just as I heard footsteps in the corridor. I kicked the shards into the corner and scurried back to my seat. From outside the door I heard the clinking of crockery shifting on a tray. The much-mentioned cup of tea was finally arriving. However, balancing a tray and unlocking a door is not easy. My instinct was to get up and hold the door open (when it was unlocked) to help, but the more critical part of me rebelled against doing anything to help my captor. Besides, I did not want her to realise that I knew the door had been locked. So I stayed where I was and prepared my most innocent expression.

The clinking became more frantic and just as I was tensing myself for the crash of a dropped tray the door flew open.

'Wretched thing,' said the woman. For a moment I thought she was referring to me, but she crossed the room and beamed at me. ''Cuse me putting this down on the floor. Derek's got the table out the back for fixing. We had a big order in recently. Derek was slaughtering day and night, so I ended up feeding the pigs. I'm all behind in the house. What must you think of us?'

I took the cup she offered me. 'I think that you and your husband run a most successful business. I am sure your produce is excellent.'

The smile grew broader. 'So you're the cook of the house. You're mighty young for such a post. Your employer is a lord, your husband said.'

My brain worked furiously. 'I wasn't meant to be the cook,' I said. 'I met Rory at the country fair, and with him being in service – well, you know how it is, we had to marry quickly if we wanted to be together. His master was kind enough to offer me a position as an under-cook. His own cook was getting on in years and he thought she could train me up over time to replace her. Only she did not take it that well.'

166

'Walked out, did she?'

'She didn't like me from the off, nor the thought of being replaced even though she was getting on in years, but when the master said he was set on coming down here it was the last straw. She said there was no way she was moving away from her people. They parted on bad terms and now the cooking is all down to me.'

I opened my eyes very wide and tried to look overwhelmed. 'The truth is, I can cook a good meal for my own family, but I am spending day and night poring over the old recipes the cook left behind. You wouldn't have a good recipe for pork belly, would you, ma'am? Only I know it's one of the master's favourites and I will have to make it very soon.'

'Oh, you poor little thing,' said the woman. 'What a pickle you're in. If I didn't have the kitchen so full of baking I'd take you through and let you copy out some of my recipes.'

'Oh, I would not mind the mess, ma'am. That would be so helpful.'

'You might not mind it, but I have my pride.'

'I do understand what with your husband being so busy.'

'Just married, are you?' she asked.

'Yes, ma'am.'

'I'm sorry to say it but you will find husbands a right trial. The things they can get you embroiled in if you take my meaning. A sweet young thing like you too.'

'I am sure Rory will know what is best for me,' I said though the words stuck in my throat.

'You be careful, dear. That man of yours is a

167

wrong 'un. Take it from one that knows. Don't you let him be leading you down the wrong path. Can happen all too easy and all too quick.' She blushed slightly and turned her face away. Then reaching into her apron pocket she produced two biscuits. 'Fancy one? I always keep a little treat by me for when I'm feeling low.'

The biscuit she proffered was large and covered with lint from her apron pocket. It looked more like the kind of thing you would feed a pig. I was spared the necessity of taking the thing as the parlour door opened and Derek stalked in, closely followed by Rory. The woman shoved the biscuits quickly back in her pocket.

'Most interesting,' Rory was saying. 'I will be happy to recommend you to my master.'

'Nothing but the best pork here,' said Derek. 'We supply the White Star liners, you know.'

'Really?' said Rory, feigning astonishment. 'That is a very high recommendation and I am even more indebted to you for taking the time to show me over your farm. Come, Effy, it is time for us to go. We have taken up more than enough of these good people's time.'

I stood up. The woman looked at her husband. Some unseen communication passed between them and Derek moved away from the door. Rory and I uttered our thanks once more and we left. It took all my effort not to run to the automobile. Rory started the engine and climbed up beside me.

'Goodness,' I said as he drove down the driveway, 'I never thought we would get through that unsuspected.'

'We dinnae,' said Rory. 'Did ye not notice they never asked the name of our master nor where our house was. They knew we were not who we were pretending to be.'

'So why did they let us go?'

'I have nae idea,' said Rory. 'And that's what's bothering me.'

Chapter Twenty-five

In which Bertram and Rory make a plan and it goes as well as one would expect

'What did you discover?' I asked.

'Not now,' said Rory. 'Wait until we are back at the hotel and we can talk freely.'

Rory drove away from the farm for some distance then looped back to pick up Bertram. He and Bertram hefted the alarmingly still carpet into the baggage compartment while I packed up the picnic things as quickly as I could. There was very little food left. Bertram must have made a real pig of himself.

We drove back towards the hotel, but rather than going directly there at one point much nearer the town Rory pulled over by a hedgerow.

'Stay in the automobile, Euphemia,' he warned.

'Yes, no peeking,' said Bertram.

I coloured deeply, thinking that both men must be going to answer the call of nature and also thinking how very much easier men have it with so many things. I crossed my legs and told myself I would be back soon. The carpet in the back moaned and shifted slightly. I sighed with relief. At least Bertram had not beaten the man to death with his shoe.

The men returned in short order. Now both of them were dressed in poor, well-worn clothes.

'What on earth are you doing?' I protested. 'The hotel will never let you in looking like that!'

'Now, Euphemia, no complaining. Rory and I have talked it over and it is the only way to deal with the situation.'

'What is?' I asked.

'You haven't told her?' asked Bertram.

'I can hardly do so with him listening.'

'He won't be able to hear anything when I close the door,' said Bertram.

Rory shot him an evil look.

'Oh yes, well, I suppose there is always a chance,' babbled Bertram. 'Better you don't know for now, Euphemia.'

I would have protested further, but Rory was cranking the engine into life and no one would have heard me. Whatever it was, the men had decided something between them and had determined that I would not like it. The chances were they were right. I felt all the fight go out of me. I had been more on edge than I realised at the farmhouse, and according to Rory it had all been to no avail. I closed my eyes and shut the world out. I felt exhausted and hopeless. Above all I felt unequal to further arguments.

We stopped. I did not recognise the road. Bertram and Rory lifted out the carpet and carried it

170

off between them. I had no idea what they had planned, but I knew they would not harm the man inside. I hoped they were going to leave their unusual delivery outside a police station. Hopefully, we were far enough away from the town of Southampton that we would not be traced by our descriptions.

It was then I saw a ship mast pass behind a tree. We were by the docks. My first thought was that we were also by the tea-shop. I scrambled down and made my way quickly across the docks to answer my own call of nature. I emerged from the tea-shop's facilities feeling much more capable of facing the world.

Then I saw them.

Bertram and Rory, the carpet slung between them, trotting up the gangplank of a cargo ship and disappearing into the hold.

I could not intervene without giving them both away, so I made my way back to the automobile. I did not get into my seat, but paced back and forth in front of the vehicle. I worked myself into a furious temper, so when I heard the ring of nailed boots behind me on the road I swung round full of angry accusations.

The words died on my lips as I saw the man who had emerged onto the road from some tall bushes. He was no-one I had ever seen before. A jagged scar ran down his right cheek like a villain out of a story book and in his hands he held a sack. I had hardly time to cry out before the sack descended over my head and my feet were swept out from beneath me.

Of course, I fought back. I kicked and screamed

171

and even tried to bite through the sack. I wiggled from side to side so much I almost fell from his shoulders. I was unceremoniously dumped on a hard floor. Then I felt a blow to the back of my head and everything went dark.

What awoke me was the smell.

'Pig shit,' said a familiar voice. 'Guaranteed to bring the most unconscious person back to the land of the living.'

Cords bound my wrists and ankles. I opened my eyes and a blinding pain shot through my head. I was lying in straw, facing a dirty wall. Light filtered in from bars behind me, making a shuttered effect.

'So what is the plan to rescue me?' asked Fitzroy. 'Knife in your boot? Dare I hope for a gun?'

'Where are we?' I asked.

'Damn,' said Fitzroy. 'Not quite the answer that I was hoping for. We're on a pig farm, Euphemia, scheduled to be pig food.'

'They must have followed us when we left,' I groaned. I began to inch myself up to a sitting position.

'You came here?' gasped Fitzroy. 'I don't know if I am more impressed by your tracking ability, your bravado, or your damn stupidity.'

I pushed myself up with difficulty on my elbows.

'How about your stupidity in getting caught in the first place,' I said. Then I caught sight of his face. His eyes were ringed with black. One was so puffed up the eye was completely closed. There was a deep cut on his cheek. Blood oozed from between his teeth. Under it all he was paler than snow. One arm hung awkwardly by his side,

172

broken. My gaze followed the arm down. The fingers on his right hand were twisted and broken. His shirt was torn open and there was blood on his chest. The cheery voice was misleading.

'Dear God,' I said. 'What have they done to you?'

'Oh, you know,' said Fitzroy, 'just a little bit of torture between friends.'

'What do they want?'

'I cannot possibly tell you that. They might still be listening and then all my efforts would be in vain.' He took a deep breath. 'I am sorry about this, my dear, but it is not going to end well for either of us.'

'What on earth do they want me for?'

Fitzroy looked down at his boots with his one good eye. 'My apologies again.'

'Oh,' I said as the truth sunk it. 'They think you will help them if they promise to let me go free.'

'I am afraid it is worse than that, Euphemia. These are very ruthless people.'

I looked at him blankly. 'I suspect,' said Fitzroy heavily, 'that they think even if torture has not worked on me if might work on you.'

'But I don't know anything,' I squeaked.

'No,' said Fitzroy. 'They will be counting on me to be the gentleman and save you from your fate.'

'But you can't,' I said.

'No,' said Fitzroy, 'much as part of me might like to, I cannot sacrifice the safety of the nation to save you, no matter what they do.' He swallowed hard here. 'Damn it, Euphemia, why did you have to get yourself caught? You're smarter than this.'

'It was not intentional,' I said shortly.

'My dear girl, you have no idea what they are likely to do to you.'

'I am not afraid of pain,' I said.

Fitzroy's voice dropped to almost a whisper.

'I fear that will be the least of it. These people are without any moral scruples.'

Chapter Twenty-six

In which Bertram and Rory cook bacon

'Maybe Rory and Bertram will rescue us,' I said.

Fitzroy chuckled. The effort obviously cost him some pain. 'Ouch, Euphemia. You do know how to keep a man's spirits up.'

'Rory told me he knew the farmer and his wife did not believe our story.'

'That's good. Does he know how to contact my department?'

'I don't think so.'

'Not so good then. You do have a way of bringing a man highs and lows in quick succession.'

'They found the man who was bribed down at the docks.'

'Ah, I did wonder how you found me. It had to be more than chance.'

'We worked it out,' I said with dignity.

'I apologise. I do not mean to belittle your achievements.'

'Sadly, they appear to have come to naught.'

'It is rather nice to have some company,' said

Fitzroy. 'You are always excellent company, Euphemia. Did you enjoy my letters?'

'The ones I have read so far were most informative.'

'I should have known you would not read ahead,' said the spy with another chuckle. 'You have such a strong code of conduct. It really is your only flaw.'

'What do we do now?' I asked.

'Wait. Pray for a miracle. I lost my knife carving one of their faces.'

'That must have been the man who kidnapped me.'

'I should have been more careful. To think I should have been luxuriating on an ocean liner. I imagine it will be in the US by now. I have had some trouble keeping track of time.'

'Of course, you do not know!' I cried. 'The *Titanic* sank. Less than one-third of the people on board survived.'

'It sank,' echoed Fitzroy hollowly. 'That's not possible.'

'It was assumed you were lost at sea.'

'That's why no one came. I was beginning to feel somewhat unappreciated... Why did you come, then?'

'You asked me to check if you were dead. The only way I could think of that meant you were still alive would be if you had not got on board the ship. So we came down to Southampton to see if we could find proof that you had got on board.'

'Wait a minute. Back up,' said Fitzroy. 'Do you mean you brought Stapleford junior and the

175

butler into my private affairs?'

'I would not be here if I had not.'

'That's not a recommendation,' said Fitzroy. 'God, what a mess.'

'Will they really torture me?' I asked. 'It felt almost as if the farmer's wife was trying to warn me.' I told Fitzroy what had happened in the parlour. 'That's good,' said Fitzroy, 'we might be able to persuade her to let you go. She doesn't sound as if she's one of the Kaiser's most loyal servants.'

'Kaiser?' I asked astonished.

Fitzroy nodded carefully. 'You have fallen into what we in the trade call a sleeper cell. The people you have met are either English or have lived in England a very long time, but their sympathy is with Germany. This farm has probably been running for decades. It is certainly a large business from what I saw of it. The Germans will have funded them in exchange for future favours.'

'Treason!' I exclaimed.

'From a British point of view, yes, but they may be descended from Germans. They may consider themselves patriots or they may merely be trying to save their skins because they are confident Germany will win the coming war.'

'Will they?' I asked.

'Hopefully British pluck will prevail,' said Fitzroy with a lopsided smile. 'But I do expect there will be a catastrophic loss of life.'

'Can't you stop it?'

'My dear Euphemia, what exactly do you think I have been doing with my life? I have no shares in banking or arms. My sole aim has been to serve His Majesty and do my best to prevent war

176

if I can. But I am afraid, my dear, sometimes there is nothing for it, but to fight.'

'Can you smell bacon?' I asked suddenly.

'You can smell it too? I thought I was hallucinating.'

Fitzroy was in no state to stand, so I began to inch myself up into a standing position using the filthy wall.

'Listen, Euphemia, this is important. If you get the chance, run. Do not think about me. Run and get as far away from here as you can.'

'I am not leaving you behind.'

'Very noble, but I am probably already dead from internal injuries. Besides, I signed up for this. You did not.'

'You are an important asset to His Majesty and as a citizen of His Majesty's Kingdom it is my duty to do my best to save you.'

'Oh you ridiculous girl,' said Fitzroy, half laughing, half angry. 'There is no way...'

He stopped as we both heard a bolt being drawn back.

'Quick, Euphemia, pretend to be unconscious,' whispered Fitzroy urgently. As I had just reached standing height there was no way I could obey before the door opened. The farmer's wife stood in the doorway. She had a kitchen knife in her hand. She threw it at me. I tried to dodge but I was tied up tight.

The knife landed at my feet and the woman vanished, leaving the door open.

'So she's not prepared to leave us to burn. Nice woman. Or weak stomach, depending on your point of view,' said Fitzroy, stretching out his leg towards the weapon and falling short. 'Don't just look at it, Euphemia, kick that knife over here.'

I managed to nudge the knife in his direction and within seconds he had managed to free himself. He cut my cords. 'Go on, get out of here.'

I put one arm round his waist and slung his other over my shoulder. He was so weak he could not resist.

'We are both leaving,' I said.

'Other side,' commanded Fitzroy. 'My left arm still works. I can throw the knife if need be.'

'I can't put your broken arm...'

'Yes, you bloody well can. If you are going to try and rescue me it will be on my terms or not at all,' yelled Fitzroy in my ear.

I did as I was bid, though I heard him grunt with pain. I headed for the door. The smell of bacon was stronger now and there were sounds of animals panicking.

'They've set the damn place on fire, haven't they, your boyfriends?' said Fitzroy. 'I hope to God they have some idea of where we are. I'd hate to have gone through all that only to end up like a kipper.'

I dragged us both out into the passageway. Fitzroy was trying to support himself as much as he could, but he was very heavy against me. We could not move quickly. I prayed that Bertram and Rory had set the fire some distance from us. There was no possibility of us being able to outrun flames if they were close by.

At the end of the passageway I could see the outside. The woman had left the door open behind her.

'Where are we?' I asked Fitzroy.

178

'At the back of the house block,' he answered. 'If you go for that door we will have to make our way around the entire building.'

'You want us to go further in?'

'Let us hope the fire has not been set too close to the house. Our best chance is the side door. It leads directly on to the driveway.'

'The way we came in. But which direction? I am all turned round.'

'That way,' nodded Fitzroy. 'Let us hope everyone else is out saving the pigs.' He gripped the knife in his hand more firmly.

We edged along the corridor. Then from up ahead came shouts. 'Back! Back!' commanded Fitzroy. 'We'll have to go out the other way.' He put on a surprising turn of speed. We made it out of the open door and into the sunlight. Fitzroy breathed heavily and almost fainted.

'Not sure I can go much further,' he said.

Behind us from the house I could hear the sound of running feet. In front of us were rows upon rows of pig pens. Smoke was drifting across them. I could not see the actual fire, but I smelled burning pig flesh. The animals were going mad in their stalls. 'Come on,' I said to Fitzroy. 'We're almost there.'

'You are a most annoying girl,' muttered the spy, and gritted his teeth, but it was clear his strength was failing. I could not hold him. He was slipping from my grasp, when miraculously Bertram appeared running round the side of the building, quickly followed by Rory.

'Help me!' I yelled. They rushed over and took an arm each to hold up Fitzroy.

'We have to go that way,' said Bertram, indicating the way they had come. 'The fire's taken hold on the other side.'

I needed no further encouragement and led the way, with the two of them half dragging, half carrying Fitzroy. Behind us I could hear footsteps. I took a turn to the left, hoping to lose our pursuers by not taking the most direct route. This proved to be a major mistake.

I ran down the row, thinking to turn at the corner, except there was no corner. We had come up against the back fence of the farm. It was wood and brick, like the sides of the sties.

'Back!' I yelled to the others, 'back!' But it was too late. Derek, plus the scarred man, and three other men looking equally fierce, blocked our exit. We were trapped.

Chapter Twenty-seven

Fire in the hold

The men advanced towards us. All of them were carrying knives. Not kitchen knives, but the kind you use for butchering carcasses. There was determination in their eyes.

'Open the pens,' said Fitzroy.

'What?' said Bertram, whose head was practically coming off, he was looking around so quickly.

'The pens. Open them.'

Rory realised before the rest of us what he

180

meant. He dashed forward and opened two of the pig gates. Four enormous pigs surged forwards and headed towards the farmhands. They were huge porkers and they were setting a fast pace. Panicked by the fire, they formed a solid flank of flesh as they advanced down the passageway. Rory moved forward, opening more and more gates. The panicked animals fled.

I expected the farmhands to retreat. Frightened pigs are not only large, but fierce. They are capable of biting and mauling. My heart was in my mouth. I prayed Fitzroy's plan would work.

'Get her over the wall,' he said to Bertram.

'But you will never make that!'

'I know. Get Euphemia out of here.'

Bertram looked from my face to Fitzroy's. Then he set the spy down on the ground as gently as he could.

'I am not leaving you,' he said. And then with strength I did not know he had, he tossed me up and over the wall.

I landed on the other side in a heap, bruised but with nothing broken.

'Come on,' I yelled. 'Come on.'

'He can't make it, Euphemia,' called Bertram. 'Rory and I will find another way out.' I jumped up and down helplessly on the other side of the wall. 'Did the pigs take those men down?'

'No,' called Bertram and I could hear how resigned he was in his voice. 'They leapt up on to the sty walls. Rory is running out of pigs. They will be coming for us soon. You need to get away.'

'I am not leaving you,' I yelled.

'Yes, you bloody are,' yelled Bertram and Fitzroy together.

I put my hands against the wall. Tears were coursing down my face. 'I am not,' I said quietly and furiously. 'I am not. There has to be a way.'

I felt a sudden tap on my shoulder.

'If you would stand back, ma'am, we will have this wall down in a trice.'

I turned to find myself facing a small group of soldiers. Two men stood behind them in suits looking remarkably calm.

'Stand away, sir,' called one of the soldier. 'Fire in the hold!'

'Hell,' I heard Fitzroy yell. 'Move, Bertram!'

The next moment the wall blew apart, throwing dust into the air and clouding my vision. The soldiers rushed in.

One of the men in suits came over to me and held out his hand.

'It is good to finally meet you, Euphemia. You are a remarkably difficult woman to follow.' I took his hand and then to my everlasting embarrassment dropped into a dead faint on the spot.

EPILOGUE

It seems that from the moment the officer from the SOE had dropped off Fitzroy's package to me at Muller House, Fitzroy's colleagues had been following me. They had not expected to find Fitzroy alive, but had taken a professional interest in whatever tasks he had left me to complete for him.

Fitzroy was livid. 'Can a man not have any privacy?' he demanded once we were safely back in a nearby house that the other spies seemed to have commandeered. A doctor had been fetched for him, and he was now a walking, or rather stumbling, mess of bandages and splints.

'I would have thought you would be glad to be rescued,' said Bertram, who had taken to lying on the sofa in what was clearly a family living room with a bandage soaked in ice-water on his head. 'I was certainly very pleased to see the fellows.'

'But to follow Euphemia when I had set her on a personal errand. My last wishes in fact. It goes beyond the bounds of common decency.'

'Something you would never do,' said Rory drily.

Fitzroy had the grace to blush slightly. 'That is not the point.'

'What will happen now?' I asked.

'They will send cleaners into the farm. It will be tidied up. Dreadful accident or some such thing. You will all return to your respective homes and I will be taken back to be debriefed for hours, days, perhaps even weeks.'

'What was this all about?' asked Bertram.

'Same thing that Scotland was about,' said Fitzroy. 'They wanted to know if the plans were going ahead.' He looked over at Rory. 'Incidentally, they are not, but that's a state secret. We are going to build extra dreadnoughts instead.'

'To where shall I return your letters?' I asked.

Fitzroy grinned. 'Keep them,' he said. 'For next time.'

Wounded as he was I threw a pillow at his head.

'No,' I said, 'never again.'

'Ah, Euphemia,' said the spy, 'you know you loved it.'

The publishers hope that this book has given you enjoyable reading. Large Print Books are especially designed to be as easy to see and hold as possible. If you wish a complete list of our books please ask at your local library or write directly to:

Magna Large Print Books
Magna House, Long Preston,
Skipton, North Yorkshire.
BD23 4ND

This Large Print Book for the partially sighted, who cannot read normal print, is published under the auspices of

THE ULVERSCROFT FOUNDATION